S. RO

Diamond Coins

outskirts
press

Outskirts Press, Inc.
http://www.outskirtspress.com

ISBN: 978-1-9772-3423-0

Cover Image by S. Rora Brown

Backgrouund Image © 2021 www.gettyimages.com. All rights reserved - used with permission.

Outskirts Press and the "OP" logo are trademarks belonging to Outskirts Press, Inc.

PRINTED IN THE UNITED STATES OF AMERICA

Contents

Foreword

In your car, at a stoplight have you ever wondered if the person in the other cars next to you will ever enter your life? Maybe a stranger for now and possibly a friend in the near future? Four women, each on a different timeline in life, sit at a four-way stoplight. Each one is at a different and special time in life.

Life is like a belly dance. In the beginning it is slow, fresh, and creative. Don't be shy. The middle is artful, fun, and sassy, working to reach for your goals, feeling playful, joy, and exuberance. The later years are controlled, serious, with strong expression and knowledge. Like life, the dance is learning to crawl before you can walk, walk before you can run or dance. The more you practice the better you become.

As a troupe, the combination of dancers, imagine the first dance would be called the entrance, just starting the journey. In the next dance, called the taxim, the melody is slowly unveiling and coming out into the world. Then the high-spirited dance, upbeat and full of energy into the core of life. Let it show what you have to offer. The drum solo follows, seriously powerful and strong, and keeps moving forward with joy. Life as a dance is a belly dance. Only stop to dance with friends. Shimmy on.

1

Lady Amisi

Five Years Ago

"Ladies and gentlemen, Lady Amisi!"
The crowd gave a standing ovation. Lady took to the stage with joy on her face and in her heart as she gazed into the crowd, all ready to perform, wrapped in her three-and-a-half-foot veil, half tucked in at her hip belt and the other half cascading over her opposite shoulder. She started dancing with one of her signature veil combinations as she floated by on the balls of her feet. Her long black hair curled all the way down past her butt. Lady had custom-ordered her dress online and the dress fit perfectly and the veil matched perfectly. Perfect. Nothing could go wrong. *I've got this!*

Not everyone was so happy.

But during her performance a bead rolled under her foot as she shifted her weight to step into a four-point spin. With her arms and veil high above her head, the round bead under her foot was just enough to make her try to adjust her footing because it hurt. It was a round bead but the pain was sharp. Something went wrong with her balance in the last spin, when Amisi shifted her arms and her veil went up in the air and her ankle first, then knee went sideways the wrong way. That alone was painful, but her knee popped out of socket! Her cry of pain was unmistakable, as she fell at the same time her veil cascaded down, over her head and face. It almost made it look like, but not sound like, she meant to do that. Like the professional she was, she stayed down and made a few hand sways and waves in the air until the end of the song, under the cloak of the veil, hiding the pain and tears on her face until the lights went down.

She called for the security men to help her off the stage because it was too painful to stand on her own, and that is when it was all too clear that she was hurt, bad. She was carried off, resting her arms over the shoulders of the two men to take the pressure off her right leg. All the staff wanted her to go to the hospital right away, gathering around her, but Lady insisted on staying until the final results were in for the winner of the competition. Lady Amisi thought that her performance was not the best for a win, but she wanted to know who was to win the elaborate, jewel-encrusted Rak Sai costume — a piece too heavy to perform in but perfect for posing, social media, and most sought-after bragging rights.

2

Shylessa

Discontented at a four way stop intersection, but the first of the four to get going and pull off, Shylessa Geris was on her way home, to her parent's home to be more exact. To describe Shylessa in one word is like her nickname, shy, but at this point in her life her mood was more melancholy. Now that she had graduated from high school, she was trying to figure out what college to go to and the all and all question, what to do with her life. It was her turn to go at the light, and she sped on in her mother's old Hyundai Santa Fe hand-me-down. The sunroof gave air and sunlight to her curly, up-cut, frosted pink short bob that complemented her toasted sugar complexion.

She was able to take a little time off from school to decide and plan her "destiny," that word on auto play back in her mind. Not finding it to be an easy assignment, burgers and ice cream seemed to soothe the daunting task that consumed her thoughts day and night. That did not go well for her waistline, she thought. At 5'5"and around 140 pounds, her weight had usually been more up than down depending on what was going on in her life at the time. And right now she still had her baby fat, so she looked very young.

Now almost twenty-one, she was the only child, and still at home with her Southern-raised, protective parents. Raised in St. Paul, Minnesota, she had been leading a sheltered life. Not an outspoken or outgoing type of young lady, she just found being in the background safer. She could play for hours on the piano; in fact that is exactly what she did with most of her downtime. She also taught piano part time to some of her St. James Church members, children, and teens for income, sometimes being called on to play the organ during church services, weddings, and other functions. She also founded and taught "The Spirits" praise dancers at her church, allowing her to make more money and keep busy. They met every Monday night. The music that they practiced "praise dancing" to was mostly drums with a touch of piano. Her childhood friend Roberta, who everyone called Bird because she didn't like her name, played the drums for the church choirs and could really make the drums tell a story, with music you could feel in your soul and tap a toe to. The slow beats created the feeling of pain or despair, then building the tempo faster, up-lifting the feeling into joy and praise with increasing intensity. She was good. And together they had a mean beat. Composing the music together gave them freedom of expression. Adding a little jazz, with R&B as well to integrate basic hymns, was always a big hit with the congregation. To stand out Shy and Bird made interpretive dance outfits for the dancers, who ranged in age from five to sixteen years old—not a hard task to the two experienced sewers. They had taken the same sewing classes in high school.

The two girls were always on the lookout for new dance styles to add extra drama to the routines. While looking on the Internet, Shylessa found "veil dancing" with one veil and two larger veils at the same time. She had seen other praise dance troupes perform with shorter, smaller versions of the veils. What she found under veils, belly dance, had the most DVDs on that subject. She ordered a couple on the art of veils and a couple of other types. When the DVDs came in, she was lucky to have the house to herself for a couple of hours, as her parents were out.

"I can watch these in peace," she said out loud, glancing at the clock on the wall.

The first section was the warmup, and she tried along. "I could afford to lose a couple of pounds," she muttered to herself. Time passed by quickly as she learned to spin without getting dizzy. "Drink plenty of water and focus on one spot in the room and bring your eyes back to that spot when you come back round." She found that advice very helpful. But the beautiful, fluid movements of the dance, especially with the veil, she found to be very exciting and fun. Something she could do more often, shimmy down some of her baby fat.

Shy called Bird to come over. All their lives living only a block away from each other. When Bird arrived she was more than happy to add something new to the same old routines that they had been doing for too long. Bird really liked the moves with the veils, but both liked all the rest of the dance too. Shimmies are basically bending and almost straightening your knees back and forth to the beat. Start out slowly at first, then increase in speed without losing the rhythm. Large hip circles to pelvic circles and undulations really worked the abs and the core, while chest circles and snake arms worked the upper body.

"Work it, girl!" they both shouted to each other's moves. At the end of the DVD, the dancer gave an extra performance in full costume; this was the first time they had seen a real belly dance performance. The veils that were used flowed like silk in the air.

"The outfits are really pretty, but a little scant for church, don't you think?" Bird said, still watching the video. Bird was a little shorter than Shy at 5'4" and always a chocolate bombshell, with natural jet black hair that she wore bone straight just past her chin.

"They are, but I think we could use the veils a little bigger than the ones the other groups use for more of a dramatic effect, right? It wouldn't take us long to make them. Just some sheer fabric, then roll the hems. We could have them done for our next meeting on Monday!" Shy was already picking up her coat. "Let's get to the fabric store now and get started tonight!" she said, almost at the door.

"Don't you think we should get approval for church funds to be used for this project by your mom?" Bird had her own money. She started working as a pharmacy technician when she turned eighteen, and now she was already twenty-one years old before Shylessa by only five months.

"No. I want this to be a surprise; I'll use my

own money. Let's get going before my mother gets home and finds something wrong with it and tries to talk us out of it."

"I'm with you, 'cause she sho will," Bird added, knowing Shyleesa's mother very well. They had been besties since before they could talk. Bird's parents were Shy's godparents. Mrs. Geris always offered to babysit since the two would cry when apart anyway.

It was early fall in Minnesota, and Halloween fabrics were sparkling and glittering in the lights cascading down on bolts for all types of costumes for Halloween and school dance programs.

"I think I will make a hip scarf out of one of these fabrics. It doesn't look that hard," said Shy.

"You look at everything like that," Bird said.

"No really, all we have to do..."

"We?!" Bird said, not wanting to take on more work.

"Yes, we. You are going to make one too. As I was saying, all we need is about a half a yard of material for a triangle, less for a rectangle hip scarf. Match the material with enough trim to go around the edges of the scarf. Something with movement for shimmys, then add some beads here and there to really add some intrest and style wahen we are working out."

Bird had already picked out her fabric while she was talking and was ready to head to the trims and beading area of the store knowing it was pointless to argue, but still sort of excited to start something different.

There was a sale going on sheer chiffon that would work nicely for the veils for the praise dancers, also three yards each for the two of them to practice with that matched their hip scarves. On the DVDs it told them to make sure they had at least six inches past their fingertips on each side. Shy picked out the fuchsia with black beads and trim and Bird picked out the turquoise with the turquoise and black beads. To keep the sheer chiffon fabric straight, the salesperson ripped the fabric instead of cutting it. And the edges did not ravel loose.

"Did you see that she ripped it instead of cutting it! That is what we will do after we measure each of the praise dancers. It will be much easier than hemming it, and keep it lightweight to float in the air." Bird had said she didn't want to sit around hemming scarves all night.

Happy with their purchases, they went back to Shy's house to start their projects. Shy's mother and father were home and found the DVDs Shy had left on her bed.

"Hello, Mom and Dad!" Shy and Bird bounded into the home not knowing what was waiting for them. When they entered, Bird had not even enough time to say hello to her friend's parents when…

"What kind of trash is this you're ordering off that no-good computer!" Shy's mother boomed. "I told your father you should be supervised when you're on that thing! What do you think you're going to do with this kind of stuff?! Huh?! Half-naked women bouncing around… that's not nice! I know you two are not trying this stuff! Well, what do you have to say for yourselves? Don't just stand there looking crazy!" She didn't even take a breath.

"Mom! Calm down! Why were you in my room, for one thing? And this is about veil moves for the praise dancers." Shy barely finished that sentence before her mother again cut her off.

"I know you two aren't going to parade around letting your stomach hang all out in public. I know you didn't just mention the praise dancers! You better think again! In church!"

"Ahhhhgh!" came from both ladies in unison.

Shy stormed to her room, and Bird followed. She didn't want her friend alone right now. Her mother stormed into her bedroom. Doors slammed in each of their rooms. Shy's father just sat there at the kitchen table, uneasy but grateful for the silence. For the moment anyway. Shylessa was a young lady now. She had been taught right from wrong. He knew his daughter. She was not the type to do something wild or disrespectful. His little princess was just growing and expanding herself. He could also see that his daughter was ready for some changes in her life, while his wife was stuck in a rut. Not wanting any change. And even with the best intentions for her daughter, she could be a little too controlling, plain and simple.

3

Tesseanna

"It is my turn , ladies," Tesseanna Ruben mumbled under her breath as she took off at the four way intersection. She was headed home to drop off her car.

She was beautiful, twenty-four years old, and out and about looking for a job to make the rent. She was 5'9" with flawless honey brown skin and not a pore in sight. Her hair was softly relaxed spiral ringlets cascading down to the center of her back, in a deep burgundy color job. A straight "A" student, her college tuition was paid for in full by scholarships, and she didn't have to worry about that, but room and board on campus would have been paid. She insisted on staying off campus in her own first apartment.

She was majoring in physical science in a Minnesota college. Maybe a career in physical rehabilitation or a personal trainer could be the job she was really after, but for now, what Tesseanna Ruben really wanted to do was dance. Dancing on Broadway was a long shot, she thought, but maybe the Guthrie Theater downtown Minneapolis, close to where she was living, would be a closer dream. Tess, as she was called by friends and family, needed money...quickly. The rent was coming up due. She had already depleted her allowance for this month from her family not that far away, living in Woodbury, Minnesota. Books weren't cheap and neither were all the other expenditures she needed to stay in school. Now it was time to stand on her own two feet. Rent wasn't going to pay for itself. She should have stayed in a dorm room, it would have been a lot cheaper, but no, she didn't want that. Now she needed to pay for that decision with some type of job to work around her classes and her study time and more importantly provide some quick cash.

Tess was lucky to have been given a car for a graduation present, a brown Buick Encore, but she was to pay for insurance and upkeep of the car. Gas prices were climbing higher and higher. Even though the car was good on gas, it was still too expensive to burn gas running around job hunting, and parking fees were out of the question, so something on the bus line would be the best way to start.

Jumping on the next bus to downtown Minneapolis to check out possible employment leads, Tess kept her eye out for something on the bus line. A sign in the window of a bar caught her eye. Waitressing could be a flexible hour type of job to work around her class schedule. Also Tess had some experience in waitressing. But the sign also read "Dancers wanted."

"Alrighty then, that sounds like it might work, what the heck," Tess mumbled to herself. She got off at the next stop and walked back to the bar's entrance.

Dancing was her strong suit. Ever since she was in high school, Tess danced in school plays and on the dance squad. The rush of adrenaline when she danced for the basketball team's half-time was a vivid forefront memory for her. With an equal counter memory of a couple of the players, not used to being turned down, chasing her and calling her "Teasing Tess!" She shook off that unpleasant memory to stay focused on the present task at hand.

When Tess walked through the door she noticed that this bar had a specific type of crowd… men. The only women she saw inside were working. They were waitressing or dancing…exotic dancing. Not exactly what Tess had in mind, but she decided to keep an open mind. She needed a job, quickly. She met the owner, Mr. Hamilton, and handed him her resume. Mr. Hamilton eyed her up and down, like she was candy or something, with a smile on his face. Tess fit the requirements for the waitress position. Even though she had no exotic dance experience, her weight of 135 pounds and height of 5'9" met the requirement for all the girls working there. Not to mention her 38D cups, tight, tiny waist, and an ice-cream scoop butt.

"I think you will work out fine as a backup dancer too," Mr. Hamilton said with a nod of approval. "You can start this weekend as a waitress."

Although Tess had tried many types of dance, exotic was not on that list. She decided to do a little research on the subject online. Tesseanna went back home and looked up "dance" on her computer. A myriad of results came up under this wide subject. Pole dancing, table dancing, and lap dancing to name a few. Most of the moves were not that unusual to her; dancing at the clubs and watching music videos, she felt as if she had seen it all in one form or another.

Some other different types of dance popped up, piquing her interest. Latin dancing was fast and very saucy. Ballroom had the most beautiful, sexy outfits from fur trim to sequins. Belly dancing came under dance and had a little bit of everything.

"A little work tightening my abs sounds like a plan," Tess admitted to herself and ordered a DVD on belly dancing and exotic dance for beginners.

The first weeks on her new job, she was shown around and waited tables. Tess was happy not having to dance on the catwalk and still stayed clear of all the tables where some of her male schoolmates sat after classes. All of the waitresses wore the same skimpy outfits, so she blended in fine. Not too many students came in on weekdays anyway.

There were classes at different times of day and for her, only one at night, so working didn't interfere with her study time.

4

Funesta

S *he looks familiar,* Funesta thought.
She was getting a little impatient waiting for her turn to go at the intersection and thinking about all of the things going on with her work day ahead, and what went on last night. Staying up late, then going to work or school early the next day was sort of the norm for Funesta Flores. In fact she felt as if her performance and creativity level thrived on the lack of sleep. Moreover, it was sort of a game to her. But at her last doctor visit came a warning, to find a way to relieve stress and to get more sleep. A spicy caramel, she was 5'7", 140 pounds, and twenty-nine years old. Her blood pressure was on the high end for one so young in an otherwise curvy, long-legged, healthy body. Now was the time to get blood pressure under control without meds and keep it under control before it became a bigger issue to deal with later.

A professional student with her BA degree now working on her MA degree, Funesta was a full-time student with a full-time job and was a late night club hopper, which didn't leave time to go to the gym, work out, or eat right. Her social life was all fun, no love. Her taste in men was very selective. He would have to match her high energy level. Fun was always at the party living one day at a time. No boyfriends, just loving life.

Her old job allowed her to travel state to state constantly. She liked that for a while but it got sort of lonely…sometimes. Her current job as manager was at a Minnesota company that made and distributed wooden canes for wholesale and retail sales. She was only able to travel once in a while to different states and sometimes out of the country to purchase exotic lumber for the company. All of the canes that were made at the company were for medical use; some special orders were not unusual, but when she came across an order for lightweight fancy canes, that got her attention. Who would use canes with no rubber tip for gripping the floor? Being so light the canes would not support the weight of most people. Fancy wood also takes longer to come back from the factory, and this order needed to be filled right away before it became late. Due date was…she paged through the work request. *It's due today!* Fun quickly got on the phone. The foreman told her the order had shipped and should arrive soon. "This order was sent here?" Funesta let him have it. "Mierda!" That meant "shit" in Spanish; she learned that from her dad. Not that he could see her on the phone, but she tossed her thirty-inch ponytail around her head, 360, and it landed on her back. It was not all hers, by about six inches. She wore her hair up in a high, slicked-up ponytail to keep it out of the way and accent her high cheekbones and when she smiled to see her dimples in her cheeks.

"This order was to be sent directly to Polished Coins Ink in uptown Minneapolis." She hung up the phone and called for one of her assistants to find the lost canes.

"This will make me look bad if we promised to deliver the order by today!" The box had arrived earlier that day and was not handled correctly. To her relief the box was found swiftly by her staff. She called and tried to have it picked up and re-sent, but the delivery date would still take it well past the original order's delivery agreement date. She was going to assign her assistant to drop the box, but then she looked at the address. "Polished Coins. I wonder what kind of company is this anyway?"

The canes were made from a very lightweight, honey-colored, simply gorgeous wood. Since it was on the way, just past one of the clubs Fun liked to hang out at after work, Fun decided to take it there herself like a responsible manager; also it looked good for getting off earlier on a Friday afternoon. Fun freshened up her makeup in the bathroom so she could go directly to the club after dropping the canes off. The canes were already paid in full, so it would be a quick in and out drop-off and then start her weekend early. Funesta called ahead to make sure where to go and let them know to expect their order on time. When she called Polished Coins she was asked, "Will you be dining with us tonight?

"No thank you," she replied. Even though she had no plans for dinner, and lunch was skipped looking for the box of canes, she realized later in fact she was very hungry. Funesta wrapped up a few more duties at work and left early to drop off the canes. It took less time to arrive at the restaurant than she thought. When she pulled up to the front of the building, she realized it was in fact a restaurant and club.

A Middle Eastern restaurant. "Okay… Still, what's up with the canes? Maybe decorations?" she wondered.

When she stepped inside the restaurant, she heard a commotion going on with five ladies sparkling head to toe in belly dancing costumes, and two men with handheld drums of some sort. Funesta overheard what the ladies were obviously upset about and ready to fight. "We can't redo that number without canes! It will not work with veils, candles, or any other props!" one of the ladies shouted.

"Then use a snake!" one of the drummers called out laughing. He was just about to be beaten up by all the ladies when one of them stopped to check out Fun walking slowly toward the group. As soon as she saw the box being carried in by Fun, she screamed!

"The canes! The canes! Thank you! Thank you! Thank you! Lady!" she called out. "The canes are here!"

"Yes, I am sorry for the delay…" Fun managed to say before the box of canes were taken right out of her hands. "I will need this order signed."

"Hello. Thank you for bringing the canes right in the nick of time." A dark-haired woman appeared from nowhere holding out her hand.

"My name is Lady Amisi. I am the owner of Polished Coins. I ordered the canes and I can sign for you," she said in a comforting voice, looking at Fun up and down. "Your name is?"

Fun extended the greeting, shaking her hand. "My name is Funesta Flores. I am the manager and assistant executive officer of Healing Woods Medical Supply Company. I apologize for the delay of your canes. What do you use them for if you don't mind me asking?"

"You are right on time." Lady put her hands on Funesta's shoulders to show there were no hard feelings after signing the form. "Please won't you stay as my guest this evening and you will see the canes in action better than I could tell you. I insist! It is the least I could do to show you my gratitude for bringing the canes to us. It promises to be a fabulous show! Let me have one of my men park your SUV." Lady wasn't about to take no for an answer. She added, "Come this way, you will dine at my table. Tell me, Funesta, have you ever eaten at a Middle Eastern restaurant before?"

"No, I have never had the privilege," Funesta replied.

"Then might I suggest trying the sample plate? It has the best of everything. Please, let's relax and enjoy. I have to tell you I haven't eaten since breakfast and I am starving." Lady pulled in her stomach. It seemed to touch her spine with a rolling wave, and her dress accented the motion by having rows of dangling beads just in the right places.

"That's amazing how much muscle control

you have! Are you a belly dancer too?" Fun's stomach felt the same way her stomach rolled.

"Yes, I have been dancing my whole life. I believe life is a dance. I love belly dancing. That's why I teach the dance upstairs on the weekends. My restaurant is an extension of me also. Eat and dance — that is joy to the soul."

The food came to the table. Fun could see the sense of pride in Lady's face as she talked about her restaurant, food, and belly dance awards she had received. It showed everywhere the eye could see. Long, flowing, satin and textured draperies made Fun feel the warmth and care that went into everything. The candles gave off soft flickering lights, and she felt beautiful. The aroma of the kitchen…she felt hungry!

"Oh my goodness, everything was delicious!" Fun sat back from the table after trying a little of everything and talking to Lady.

"I hope you will become one of our regulars." Lady smiled at Fun. "Well, time to get things started." Lady stood. "If you will excuse me." Lady curtsied and disappeared.

Just about that time the music started. The musicians took their place along the sides of the stage that was hidden behind some of the flowing draperies. When the curtains went up, there was a figure facing away from the audience in a beaded, figure-forming, beautiful dress hitting all the curves just right. It was Lady, the master of ceremonies.

"LADIES and gentlemen, welcome to Polished Coins!" The musicians made a drum roll with a little kick to it. "Tonight we have the polished troupe called SWAYSA! And the DESERT BLING."

On cue, the dancers appeared on the stage from their hidden places underneath veils that matched the stage so at first glance they went unnoticed. The crowd cheered, whistled, and woo wooed! The five dancers, all barefooted, swirled veils all around like extensions of their arms, effortlessly and flowingly. The veils matched the costumes they wore, cascading up and down like silk in the air. "Ohhhh!" Fun was startled by a flying bead that came from one of the shimming dancers' dresses. The sound the band played was wistful and playful as the dancers circled one another going in and out with a cascade of veils in the air, then in a swirl around their ankles. Another dance move was over the shoulders, then whisked away at each drummer, who playfully dodged the onslaught of veils coming at each of them from the dancers in a playful dance, or could be that they were still mad about the snake comment made earlier by the drummers. But the beat kept right on. Then to Fun's surprise, the canes that she had brought to the dancers were placed on the stage during the dancers' solo performances. The canes were wrapped in a light sheer ribbon on the curve.

Fun was on the edge of her seat. The dancers were dressed in yellow and black belly-baring one-sleeve tops; just the beading alone must have weighed the dancer down by at least a couple of pounds. Not to mention the weight of the beads on the hips from the hip belt that accented every hip movement with sparkling waves of light. There were lots of hip movements. Some of the movements looked familiar to Fun, who was no stranger to dancing. Lady looked over at her guest to see her dancing in her seat, mimicking the dancers on stage; she smiled, as she could tell Fun would make an excellent student.

5

Seri

"I think I have seen those ladies before," Seri said to herself, talking about the three other cars that were before hers. Okay with going last at the four way intersection but feeling a different ache in her shoulder than anything she had ever felt before. Seri pulled off from the stop and headed for home. Comfort and stability, that is how her friends would describe Seri S. Danbury. At this point in time, her husband, Thomas, would just call her crazy. Both retired early, both as CEOs from major companies, hers close to home, and his based out of the country. Now the couple found themselves empty nesters, and it was not the way either thought it would be. Stable but not comfortable.

Life had gone exactly the way Seri planned it. With her two babies all grown up and out on their own now, she and her husband thought that they could relax, do what they always wanted. Nothing, nice and sweet nothing. But that was not going the way she planned. They found themselves arguing over tiny things, if talking at all.

The house was large enough to escape each other, so communication was not often and with no clarity. Large rooms with vaulted ceilings and the decor were just the way she wanted.

He let her design everything. Except for his "man cave," where he spent most of his time. Like ships passing in the night they both had their own part-time jobs, training for her and field support for him. They didn't really need the money, just kept them busy. The girls both attended college with full scholarships, with one in her last year of college and the other who found a good job right after her associate degree. All they needed was help once in a while from Mom and Dad. No big deal and hardly unexpected.

As soon as Seri arrived home, she and Thomas greeted each other with a peck on the lips and in minutes started arguing, not sure what it was all about or how it got started. That was always the way it went. Seri stood about 5'4" with a powerhouse body. "Hips for days," her husband commented with love on his wife's body. Seri kept her waist trainer on, even years after having her baby girls. Her husband also loved her small feet and that she could walk on the balls of her feet after being in heels all day long.

Suddenly Seri felt numbness in her whole

right arm. It started with her fingers and went up her arm. She figured she could shake it off. She did shake it off and it went away, so she went on like nothing ever happened. She knew neither of them had eaten dinner yet.

"Maybe that's why he's acting like a fool," she mumbled to herself as she headed for the kitchen and he headed upstairs. She went to the refrigerator to take out a couple of steaks to put on the table grill. She yelled to her husband.

"Do you want a steak or leftov…?" Suddenly this time a sharp, stabbing pain crossed her neck and chest. She dropped the steaks and the barbecue sauce on the floor. She paused and took a couple of short breaths and then the pain subsided but was not totally gone. Not really knowing what to do, she reached to recover the rolling bottle on the floor. The bottle seemed to distort and blur. A sudden surge of fear came over her. She knew the warning signs of a heart attack or stroke; the leading cause of death in women was from heart attacks, and the warning signs were different from men's.

She called out with all she could manage, "TOM! …HELP ME," except it didn't come out that way; her mouth wasn't working right. She did remember to take an aspirin, which might help her if it was a heart attack, and she knew he kept a bottle of baby aspirin in the kitchen cabinet on the other side of the large kitchen. The floor was twisting and everything looked wavvvvvy. She took two steps and the floor came up to meet her.

Tom was still fuming with her, about what he was not exactly sure. Thomas had heard her call him the first time, but he didn't want to fuss anymore. He couldn't understand what was the second part she said. But then he thought he heard something about a steak? He was hungry. Did she want him to go get something? After all that fussing, she could go get something on her own!

I'm hungry too…always thinking about yourself… I'm tired too!

"Now what you say?" he yelled downstairs. "What you want now? I can't hear you! Are you still in the kitchen?" He listened for an answer as he started down the staircase and into the kitchen.

"OH! There you go again, starting some more mess with me, going to make me come all the way back down these stairs just to start something. Well look, I'm hungry and I'm not in the mood! Now what you say, girl… Seri!" he screamed when he saw she was on the floor.

6

Shylessa

Shylessa's father knew his daughter well enough to know what she would and would not do. This was not the first time he was in the position of being the middleman. The mediator whether he liked it or not. Of course he had to be the one to step in and patch things up between his girls. But which one first? His baby girl would give him the answers to the questions he was sure her mother was going to ask him. Straight answers were what he needed to calm his wife's fears. He got up only after he finished his coffee. He knocked on his daughter's door. He could hear a lot of mumbling and shuffling around from behind the door. He assumed that they thought he might be her mother knocking, so he offered, "Shy, it's me, let me talk to you two first." He was immediately let in.

"Dad! Why do you stand by and let her do things like this to me? I have done nothing wrong and she goes through my stuff like nothing! I feel like I have done everything wrong. Everything has to be the way she wants it. I have a life to live myself, you know. I have feelings too!" Shy finally took a breath and plopped down into her bean bag. "Okay, okay! Calm down and tell me something about all these belly dancing DVDs. What are they for?"

Bird answered for her friend. "Those are teaching aids for working with veils for the praise dancers. And they are very tasteful new movements for working with larger veils only. And one more thing, we, not the praise dancers, are working on burning off a little fat around our waistlines." Bird finished with a tug at the baby fat rolls around her waist.

"Sounds fine to me, just don't have your belly hanging out and everyone should be okay with what you're doing. I love and trust both of you." He reached out to the girls for a group hug and added, "Now I can go calm your mother down. Be good, ladies." And he was out the door. A good strategic move not wanting to answer the question of why they were in her room in the first place.

"Let's start on the veils," Shy said finally after pulling herself together. "All we have to do is rip the veils to the length we need."

That went rather quickly and they were done in no time.

"We need to get ready for rehearsal for the praise dancers. I also think we need a new routine using the larger veils," Shy stated, putting in a new DVD to play, using what they watched and the music to choreograph to keep the beat and story line.

1. First happiness: veils floating overhead and back, all smiles.
2. Then despair: covering up in the veil, unseen and hiding.
3. Making it through: floor work, this move has already been done, with the shorter veils, prayer hands with veil on shoulders, with a swaying movement.
4. Transforming: turning the veil around the body and letting go of one end so the dancer beside can catch it and walk in a circle, forming a ring.
5. Finale: letting go of fears, breaking the circle, dancers open the veils up and cascade them up in the air in front of themselves, and at last letting them go to float down as they pose in praise.

The larger veils conveyed more emotion and drama.

When Sunday came, the praise dancers performed the routine with grace and precision. The church gave them a thunderous applause. After church the dancers couldn't wait to learn more veil movements. Also the dancers said their shoulders felt stronger and more toned as a bonus. Shy and Bird were very proud of themselves. Even Shy's mother commented on how tasteful and elegant the new updated veils looked. Shy took that as an apology. The response to their "tool of expression" as someone commented about the bigger, better veils was even more than they could have expected. They went home and got right to work on the next routine.

"I'll get the popcorn," Shy said, heading for the kitchen.

"I'll put in the DVDs; I might as well work out along with them to burn off more baby fat," Bird confessed.

"I would love to make a whole outfit," Shy said, returning with the hot microwave popcorn.

"What! Where would you wear it?"

"Nowhere but here. It just makes the workout more fun and a little more theatrical." Shylessa also felt feminine and ladylike, like a woman not a girl. "Besides, I saw a dress that doesn't have the belly out at all. And it said somewhere that you don't have to have your belly out anyway to dance."

"Maybe your mom should try it," Bird sarcastically said and they both laughed knowing that that was not about to happen. Ever.

Shy was still moping around a little about her mother's outburst and then snooping around her room; she really didn't like that at all. Shylessa thought it was just plain rude. Although Shy tried not to show it, Bird could see right through her and offered a suggestion with skepticism.

"Maybe if she knew more about belly dancing, she might chill a little, you think?" Bird put it out there anyway, not believing it.

"I don't know, maybe one of the oldest forms of dancing. From what I read, it's a dance made by women for women as a way to alleviate the pain of childbirth and regain strength afterward." Shy stood like she was giving a speech. "It is natural to a woman's bone and muscle structure. The dance mostly focuses on isolating the torso, no matter your size or age, and with low impact to your joints. Now on YouTube some men are doing it too. There is a lot to read about it, IF she wanted to."

"I think she just doesn't want you to start dancing with snakes and doing black magic!" Bird made wiggly magic fingers at her friend.

"Now what would black magic have to do with belly dancing? And SNAKES…not me. Ain't no worries there. But it sounds like something she might worry about. I love the way the veils float, just like wings. Or wrapping up into an envelope and peeking out with grace and a little drama."

Shy picked up a veil and twirled around the room. She stopped and watched more of the DVD, the candle balancing in one hand and on the top of the head.

"I will try this; it looks like fun. Watch this as I bring this cup of water around and down and around without spilling a..." Oops! The glass didn't just spill; it completely emptied on Bird's head with a thud. "I'm sooooo sorry! Are you okay?" Shy looked around for a towel.

Bird put her hand up with a nod of her wet head, wiped her eyes enough to stand up and head for the bathroom for a towel. When Bird came back from drying herself off, she sat on a dry towel. "I think it's time to get back to coming up with a new routine," she said.

"I think it's time for me to get my own place. I'm moving out." Shy spoke her thoughts out loud, surprising herself and her friend.

"What! Your mom will freak!" Bird said, considering the consequences of a major upset in the whole household.

"She freaks all the time about everything

anyway—what's new with that! I need my own space. I've saved up enough money, I think, for a down payment on an apartment. And I can still go to school on my grants and scholarships, so what's stopping me?" Shy turned and sat down in front of her friend.

"Your mom," Bird answered. "She wants you to…"

Shy cut off Bird in mid-sentence.

"Whatever…whose life are we talking about, mine or hers? I finally found something I want to do. It's different, it's exciting, and she and her friends should follow my lead and live a little! That's it, I am starting my search tomorrow!" Shy crossed her arms in determination mode.

"Yeah, well, there is one thing you should consider when looking for your apartment," Bird said, trying to get a word in.

"Yeah, what's that?" Shy said, ready to take on any disapproving rebuttal her good friend could dish out.

"You need to look for a two-bedroom in a nice neighborhood. I don't want to live anywhere that's dangerous." Bird gave her friend a big hug.

Shy felt joy, relief, and excitement that Bird volunteered to move in with her.

7

Tesseanna

Rushing to class almost late, again, Tesseanna turned the corner into the hallway to her class when... Wham! slammed right into someone who was also not paying attention to where they were going.

"I'm so sorry" came from both parties involved in almost perfect unison as both went right for their papers, pencils, and books now jumbled together on the floor.

The first glance up was his. He had almost stopped collecting his things, stopping to stare at whom he had bumped into. Next it was her turn, wondering why whoever had almost come to a complete stop getting their stuff out of her stuff, she stared into his eyes.

Students in the hallway at the time of the crash could almost feel that their help was not needed and kept going. Only a couple of girls paused long enough to watch the two in a stare with their hands still going through papers. Under his thick lashes his eyes were gray and brown or brown and gray, she couldn't decide which. Tess lowered her gaze after feeling a blush come over her face. After the last piece of paper was finally picked up, Tess had a second to glance at the rest of him. Standing up now, she could tell he knew his way around the gym. Her eyes rolled over his strong, wide shoulders that tapered to a slim, tight waist. He had some tight abs under that shirt. He was around 6'2", white with almost black straight hair, slightly spiked. His mustache and beard were smooth against his lip and squared chin, and he did stand out from the crowd. Oh yeah, he worked out to keep that shape, she bet to herself.

The class "dong" rang, signaling the start of class and interrupting her thoughts. A couple of more sorrys and thank yous as they separated each other's papers and things and rushed to their different classrooms before the second chime. She knew she would see him again, hopefully. Tess made it to class just in time before doors were locked. Daydreaming during class was almost impossible to stop. She kept seeing his eyes, those gorgeous eyes.

"Snap out of it, Tesseanna!" she finally had to mumble to herself to get through the class assignments the teacher was going over for lab. She needed to focus on her job at hand, which was her bread and butter class. Tess's class lasted longer than his, as there was no one in the hallways, and she found herself hoping to see him somewhere in the school. Oh well, she thought to herself, maybe next time she would get to this class a little earlier. But for now it was time to focus. Forward march to the library! If she turned in the bonus work on time she would stay well ahead of the class and keep her GPA at a steady and comfortable 4.0. Thank God that her school tuition was paid for with scholarships.

While she moved through rows and rows of books in the school's library looking for the call number on a book for required reading, Tess, feeling warm, felt as if she was being watched. She turned to reach for a book and out of the corner of her eye, someone was standing just to the right of her… She jumped just a bit.

"Sorry if I startled you, again."

It was HIM! He held her gaze, and she felt a deeper warming sensation as he reached for her hand that had been frozen in midair by the surprise meeting.

"I hope you are all right," he said, still holding her hand.

"Yes, I'm fine. Thank you. I'm sorry, I will allow myself more time to get to class from now on, sorry again," she whispered.

"Are you studying to be a doctor?" he said, noticing the section of books she was in.

"Maybe one day or a physical therapist," she answered shyly.

He thought he would break the ice more.

"My name is Richard Webb," he said with a smile, shaking her hand.

Tesseanna thought she was shot by cupid's arrow because she thought she heard singing when he said his name.

Rick saw that she was surprised by the outburst from his choir outside the library and chuckled a little. "You can definitely call me Rick. The choir is rehearsing outside for an upcoming talent show later this year." He gestured to the window.

"Yes, I was wondering. My name is Tesseanna. What are you studying for?"

"Oh, I'm not a student here. I am a teacher in the arts building across the street. I am a substitute teacher once in a while here at the school, like today. I teach choir, dance, math, and music. For the upcoming show I am in charge of, I would like a wide mixture of talents to showcase. I would love for you to participate in the show. I know you can dance," Rick said with a smile and jazz hands.

She thought maybe he had seen her at the club where she worked; maybe he thought she was an exotic dancer. She looked at him, searching for the answer in his eyes.

"You definitely have a dancer's body," he said with a smooth look. "Maybe we could go out dancing sometime. Are you free this weekend?" he said, very sure of himself.

Sort of shocked by his suaveness, she had the weekend off from work but she did have the paper to write for one of her lab assignments.

"Yes, I'd like that." She surprised herself. "Saturday night work?"

"Saturday it is. I'll pick you up around six o'clock for dinner first."

The two exchanged numbers before he left.

Tesseanna tried to study in the library for a while but she kept thinking about him, so she took her work home and tried to complete her assignment there. That didn't quite work either. She couldn't focus on the task at hand. She wanted to get her hair done and her nails. *What am I going to wear?* She started to work herself into a tizzy.

"Well, if I keep this up I won't be able to go at all." She decided to finish her work and work on herself in the morning.

The next morning she started out early to a local thrift store. She found it to be the perfect place to shop when she was low on dough. She found a blouse to die for and searched for a skirt to go with it. She came across a gorgeous chiffon skirt with a beautiful belt that looked more like a belly dancer's beaded belt. There was a small tear in the skirt so it was marked down accordingly, which made it very reasonable. Tesseanna didn't notice until she got home that the skirt had a matching beaded wristband to go with it because of a phone call from her job to come into work tonight because they were short staffed. That interrupted her shopping fun and abruptly cut it short.

A Friday afternoon rush hour and the place was jumping with after the game goers. As soon as Tess entered the door, she saw him. It was Rick.

"Oh NO, I don't want him to see me!" She kept her back to him and his friends until she quickly entered the back, near the stage door and the restrooms.

8

Funesta

One by one, out of a spin each dancer picked up a cane that had that added feature, a ribbon to match the outfits tied on the end curl of the cane. Funesta watched the canes spin like batons in the air. Hand ripples made the canes twirl effortlessly. Funesta watched joyfully, and added a "Whooooo" to the interactive crowd's shouts.

After the show, Lady Amisi introduced Fun to the dancers backstage. A couple of the dancers tried a few beaded hip belts on Fun just for, well, fun. Showing her how to hold a cane was not as easy as it looked.

"Funesta, please join me for a free month's worth of lessons. I teach every Saturday at 11:00 a.m. upstairs at the club," Lady suggested.

"I think I might just do that, thank you," Fun agreed. "My doctor would be pleased to hear that I am going to do something to lower my blood pressure."

"Absolutely, dance is an excellent way to relieve stress. And the best reason I think it puts you back into the 'curve' of things," Lady said while following the curve of her waistline with her hands down to her hips, and then walked Funesta to the door. "You drive safe and see you tomorrow!" Lady waved goodbye.

On the way home Fun drove past one of the clubs she had planned on going to tonight, and slowed down. "Nothing in there will match what fun I just had," Fun said to herself and went on home to get some good beauty sleep.

In class the next morning, Funesta really did feel more vibrant than normal.

"Must have been all that extra sleep. Normally I go to bed late and then get up too early." The beginner's class didn't really challenge her enough. Fun was having fun. The moves were reminiscent of the old school dances. The full hip circle was in fact the "bus stop" in slow motion to her. And the hip locks, well, if you did that with someone else, it would look a lot like the "bump." And the reason her shoulders were nice and tight was because of "The Flirt,"' which was exactly the shoulder shimmy, her all-time favorite dance move. The hour flew by. Lady came over to Fun after the class and asked her to stay for the advanced class.

"If you think I could handle it, I'll try it!" Fun

beamed. She wasn't ready to stop anyway. Lady was pleased that Fun was picking up the techniques so easily. The advanced class took it to the next level. All classes start with a warm-up, but this warm-up added layers of turns and basic movements together.

"All right, ladies, it's time to dance!" Lady Amisi said, walking over to the wall of mirrors to change the music. "Let's all come up to the mirror and we will do a basic step for the count of six, hip bump for two, turn face front into camel walk to the right, and layer an undulation on the camel walk to the left and shimmy."

Lady knew it was much for a beginner; it was a test for Fun. The challenge was accepted. Fun was up for it. To Lady's surprise, Fun was right on count up to the hip bump. The turn was a bit wide but that was being picky, still on the count of six to the right. But what was unexpected was her undulation done with the shimmy, layered on top of the camel walk.

Fun didn't know that it was an advanced move until the end while she was standing and waiting for more of the routine. Lady wasn't the only one to notice. A few of the advanced members noticed; some were from the troupe who danced last night at the club. They let her know that she was a natural for someone who had never belly danced before. She just nailed a definitely advanced layering move.

All Lady could say was "I knew it." She went to get the canes.

"We will now show our new student some of our cane combinations, with the canes her company makes for us!" Lady informed the other girls in the class.

"The canes we ordered are a lightweight wood not found where you would find medical canes. They have no rubber tips and should fit the dancer's height, not to leave out balance for spinning and twirling." She went on. "Hold it firm so you don't let it go and hurt someone in your audience; stay in control as you twirl it through your fingers."

As Lady watched Funesta practice with the cane, she made mental plans for this natural dancer. Funesta would make a beautiful addition to the troupe. Fun noticed Lady watching her with a grin on her face.

"What? Am I doing it right?" Fun inquired.

"A bit more work on the twirl to make it effortless, but you are a quick study and I know you will have it down, just a matter of practice. Practice with this cane this week. And come next

Saturday for class. And then if you can, please come back tonight for another show this evening." Lady didn't want to push her too much. Funesta agreed to come back for the show. Fun went home after a couple of stops.

In her building there was a fitness room with a couple of stair steppers, running machines, and some other machines to work a body out. One wall was totally mirrored with plenty of room to dance in front of. She brought in her CD player and a CD that she purchased at the restaurant. For a hip scarf she used a scarf she had in her closet, and the cane that Lady let her borrow for a while. She put the music on and tried to remember the moves she had just learned in order. She was most intrigued by the cane dance, so lively and upbeat. She really got into the music.

Funesta didn't notice that she had an audience watching her. A set of dark brown eyes. The eyes belonged to a fellow tenant named Afton Bernett.

How could he have missed seeing her before? he wondered, not taking an eye off of her. He knew what floor she lived on by the type of key she had forgotten in the fitness room door keyhole. He liked the way she moved so gracefully. He heard a noise behind him, and turned to see what it was. It was only a cat running down the hall. When he looked around to see her dance some more, she had stopped and was looking at her CD player. Then she picked up a cane. Suddenly he felt like a peeping tom, intruding and shameful. But then he remembered the forgotten keys in the door, which gave him a reason to interrupt her. He turned the knob and entered the room with an "Excuse me." Suddenly music filled the room. Their eyes met. He went to her and she to him. They started to dance around and around. A warm glow came over his face. Her face came closer to his face; her lips were perfect, her nose so cute. He felt her hands on his cheeks, so soft, warm, and caring. He heard their children in the background giggling. But how was this possible?

9

Seri

His Seri on the floor? His life, his wife! One of the strongest women he had ever known. This couldn't be happening!

Seri was semi-conscious, realizing she was in an ambulance. She could hear her husband. "Seri! Wake up, girl! I love you! I'm sorry, don't leave meeeeee!" he wailed. He wanted to get into the ambulance with her, but they told him there was no room. More like he was too loud. He could follow behind them in his own car. She was stable and he had saved her life, so calm down.

She was drifting in and out of consciousness. She felt so tired.

At the hospital she was asked a few health questions. She did the best she could. Her mouth was heavy on one side, so it was difficult to speak. She was told that her husband was there and that he called their children and that a few tests were going to be taken to see if she had had a stroke or a heart attack.

"Thank God your husband was there to call an

ambulance when he did. I don't think you would have made it," one of the doctors told her. She drifted off into a drug-induced dream of the time when they first met…

They bumped into each other at a college homecoming party, literally; they were in a soul train dance line doing the bump. He always told her that was why he "fell in love with those hips." He liked to work out with weights. Standing at 6'1" to her 5'4" he would pick her up by her hips to kiss her. He was so dark and handsome. And so smart to make the dean's list. In their senior year they were married before the birth of their first daughter. Seri would have graduated early but still graduated on time. He graduated best in his class and had a good job waiting for him. She stayed home during the day and went to night school to get her master's before their second daughter was born. His job had him traveling a lot, so working was not an option for her for a while. With piano, dance, and tennis practice for the girls, not to mention hair salon appointments, braces, PTA meetings, and housework, time was sparse. They moved around with his job, and the bigger the house meant the more cleaning time. She put herself last; the girls came first, then her husband. When the girls were in high school she started working part time outside of the home.

Part time gave way to full time. Now young ladies, their daughters adored their father and demanded all of his free time whenever he was home. He denied being a big softy when it came to his ladies. Between school events, work, and home there was not much time for herself, or her husband. Now both girls were out of the house, and it seemed so quiet.

When she woke up this time she looked around the room. She was in a quiet hospital room. A large window gave her the view of the downtown St. Paul area that she knew well. A big vibrant picture of a vase of flowers and a stack of envelopes sat on the bedside table. She wondered how long she had been there. She tried to reach for the stack of get well cards, but her hand was too weak and shaking to pick them up and she dropped most of them on the floor. At that same moment the nurse came into the room.

"Oh good, you're awake. I need to take your vitals now." The nurse rolled a cart into the room with her. "I know there are a couple of family members who would really like to talk to you right now, but we can get this done now and you can have some time with them without rushing." The nurse continued her work. Seri found it hard to keep quiet during the tests that the nurse tried to finish.

"How long have I been in here? And what is wrong with me?" Seri whispered, still feeling a little weak, twisting in the hospital bed.

"Your doctor and family will fill you in on everything after I'm finished with these tests. Are you in any pain?" the nurse asked, continuing on with her work.

"No not really, just a little groggy with a slight headache," Seri admitted, putting the palm of her hand across her forehead.

"Your blood pressure is a little high still, and I need to start you on a new IV." The nurse had just finished her sentence when Tom entered the room. He paused to knock on the already opened door only after he saw the nurse in the room. His eyes searched the situation to see if it was okay for him to enter. But not waiting for an approval and not taking his eyes off his wife, now that she was awake, he entered anyway and draped himself over her without a word and held her deep in his embrace, whispering, "I love you, I love you. Thank you, God. He knows how much I love you! I've been a fool! And almost lost you!"

"I will come back later," the nurse whispered and left the room, sensing the need for them to be alone.

10

Shylessa

"It's Saturday! Let's start looking for an apart-ment today!" Shylessa exclaimed.

"Then we can go get something to eat," Bird said, starting to feel the excitement too.

"You know what they say, location, location, and location. Something on the bus line or light rail to get back and forth from school and work," Shy added.

While they were looking for apartments with availability signs, they noticed a restaurant with belly dancing on certain nights of the week.

"Look over there! That's a restaurant we need to check out," Bird said while still trying to keep an eye on the road.

"Belly dancing? Let's go there for something to eat tonight after we check out this one apart-ment. Remember this street so we can find it lat-er," Shy said.

The third apartment they looked at was just what they had been looking for. A little pricey though. Keeping that one in mind, the ladies headed for the restaurant but did put a holding fee down on the apartment. They felt like celebrating their new venture even though nothing was finalized.

"Okay, where is it…over there, did you see that? It said there are three free trial lessons."

Finding a good parking spot almost right in front of the Polished Coins Restaurant, they realized it didn't look too crowded or very fancy but very inviting.

"Let's try it out and see what it's like," Shy said, going inside.

The ladies went from not being thrilled with the outside of the restaurant to jaw-dropping, five-senses delight.

Their eyes had to adjust ever so much to the dim candle lighting, but it was so worth it. Silky fabrics flowed on the walls at the candlelit tables. The focal point of the restaurant, besides the colored mirrors behind the long, oval bar, was the dual curtain-draped stage. Drum sounds from the small group of men—you could tell they were just practicing from the start and stop of music—what a beat! The aroma of food made both of them even hungrier than before they walked in. After they were seated, a gorgeous tall lady with long black hair and a small waistline accented with a hip scarf came over to their table.

"Good evening, ladies. Namaste, my name is Lady Amisi. I hope you enjoy your dinner and the show we have tonight. Have you been to my restaurant before?" Lady smiled from one to the other.

"Thank you, and no, this is our first time. Is there any information about the belly dancing classes that are offered for free lessons?"

"Yes, I can help you with that," Lady offered.

"Are the lessons offered here?" Bird asked.

"Yes, on the upper level there are workout studios and a smaller stage than the main one in the restaurant's center. I am happy that you are considering taking classes in belly dancing. It is the best way to learn and grow in the dance. I look forward to teaching you both," Lady said.

"You're the teacher too?!" both said in unison even though neither was really shocked. This woman had an aura about herself: strong, elegant, obviously a good businesswoman.

"Yes, I am, ladies; I can't wait to see what you two can do on your own," Lady said and added nodding at Shylessa, "You two would make lovely dancers."

Bird spoke up. "I would love to try the drums. They look like fun!" She gestured to the group of men still giving a show of talent by taking turns on each other's drums.

"Maybe both? You like the music? Do you play?" Lady asked Bird.

"I do play drums but not like the ones that they are playing on," Bird admitted.

"Well, we shall see," Lady said and with that she was off with a nod of her head.

After the girls checked out the menu and put in their dinner orders they checked out the décor of the restaurant more. Shy noticed that they had a very nice table near the stage, and they would be able to see everything from where they were. She also hoped that there would be veil dancing so she could take some suggestions back to the praise dancer routines. Her focus went back to her friend when she noticed the group of drummers looking over in their direction.

"Bird, are you really going to try out those fancy drums?" Shy asked her friend, trying not to startle her. "Because I think they want you to go over there with them. Too late, here comes one of them now!"

They were all very handsome. A couple of them were just about their age. The one on the way over was in their age group or maybe a little older, with dark black hair and a tight waistline. His eyes were simply gorgeous. He was smooth as he came to the table and asked, with an accent, which one of them wanted to try the drums with him.

"Oh my goodness, what did I do!" Bird said nervously, frozen in her seat. "That was me," Bird said in a little meek voice.

"Wonderful!" He smiled, gazing into Bird's eyes. "May I invite you to take a closer look before we begin our next set?" He smiled a big, sexy, "I've been waiting for you," melt-in-your-chair smile.

Liking that smile, she replied this time with something a little sassier.

"I'd like that…a lot." There was no way to resist those gorgeous eyes, not to mention the outstretched hand to help her out of her seat.

"If you will excuse us," he said and they were off. He tucked Bird's hand under his tight bicep and whispered something into her ear as they walked away. He definitely took his time walking over to the drum group, Shy noticed. She happily watched her friend obviously flirt with her new drum teacher. The food came while Bird was still trying out a drumbeat. Bird signaled to her friend she knew and was reluctantly escorted back to her seat. He kissed her hand and returned to his group.

"Well? What did he say? How old is he? Is he

taken? Nope, he couldn't be. You two were very close together. Details! I need details!" Shy was literally on the edge of her seat.

Bird was noticeably glowing when she sat down.

"First he asked me my name and if I had a boyfriend," Bird said, still smiling.

"Ooooo, a personal interest question. Keep going." Shy could not contain her excitement for the look of coolness. "What did you say?"

"I told him he could call me Bird and that no, I didn't have a boyfriend. He must have really liked that answer because he called me Lady Bird after that and didn't let go of my hands. He did let me play a few beats on his drum, which he called a maktoum. And his other drummers wanted me to tap on their drums for luck, I think. One of his friends said something like, 'Love's first glimpse and music go together like the beat of the heart.'"

They both sighed in unison. That was a short-lived moment, as just then the drummers started a full-on dueling percussion set, and the whole restaurant got into the groove.

Bird looked over to catch the eyes of her new friend. He smiled; she smiled. He kept drumming. She, however, wasn't eating, too busy smiling at him. Shy noticed all the smiling going on and tried to interrupt a bit so he could concentrate on his job and Bird could eat.

"I think we should take those lessons this weekend, don't you, Bird?" After a few moments of silence with no answer from her friend, she tapped the table near her.

"Huh? What?" Bird was totally distracted and twisting her hair around in a curl with her fingers, something Shy hadn't seen her friend do in a long time, so she decided to let her have her moment.

While Bird was busy smiling Shy enjoyed the food and checked out the other patrons. Looking around the room she noticed a lovely couple enjoying each other's entrée and another couple staring into each other's eyes. *Must be nice to be in love*, she thought.

Lady, the owner of the restaurant, introduced the next group of performers as a troupe and soloist. "Swaysa and the Swaying Gems." The dancers came out after the huge curtains parted and the inner sheer curtains rolled up. Each of the five dancers had beautiful sheer veils each matching their costumes. They seemed to float across the floor. The veils swayed in the air back and forth, caught in the air, floating like silk clouds.

"They must be real silk to float like that," Shy said. "Not like the polyester crepe we use."

A nice move the girls noticed was a move called the "envelope," where the dancer encloses herself inside the veil and can shimmy and also bring one side of the veil down to the shoulder and slide one arm out of the veil with arm sways and bring the veil back up over the head. Shy felt that she could join in with them since she had been studying the DVDs she ordered online. They really looked like they were having fun. Bird was enjoying herself too, tapping on the table like she knew what she was doing, mimicking what her drummer friend was doing, more like it, and of course still smiling.

"The costumes are just gorgeous!" Shy said. "I wonder where they got them? The beading is so intricate and exquisite."

Bird leaned over and asked, "Could you make something that detailed?"

"I'd love to try. I wish I could dance like that. I wish I had a shape like that to dance like that!" Shy laughed.

11

Tesseanna

When Tess reached the doors of the club and entered, she heard a laugh—his laugh maybe—and quickly looked back to see if he was laughing at her. He wasn't. He hadn't seen her at all; lucky for her, he was still talking to his friends. Her waitress attire had been designed to look like a chambermaid's, so she blended in with the other waitresses and worked the other side of the club. All was fine until her boss, Mr. Hamilton, came out to the club from the back. He was counting his acts for the night and came up short a couple of dancers due to the flu. He told his head dancer to pull Tesseanna off the floor and get her ready for her dance short. Which meant that she only had to dance for one song and go back to waiting tables, just enough time to give the next dancer a break and time to get ready to go on again.

On the way backstage Tess started making up excuses not to dance. Nothing worked. She even thought about quitting, which was out of the question. She needed the money to pay bills. Tess peeped through the curtains to see where Rick was, hoping with all her heart he would leave. One of the main dancers was up and she had the crowd up and cheering on their feet, putting money into her bra and G-string. Rick was still there with even more of his friends, but he seemed to be on the phone. She had an idea. Tess thought of a way to do what she needed to do, with a twist. Maybe with some magic. In the dressing room, she noticed a beaded top and harem pants in a sheer fabric. She remembered something from the DVDs she ordered online. A whole wall full of different accessories from head to toe was available for her to pick from. Tess was up next, and she needed to change fast.

Her uniform had a short skirt, a little apron, and a tiny lacey poof pinned into the hair. When she applied for the job she wasn't very good at pole dancing; that's why working the tables worked for her. But obviously her boss had other plans for her.

She had been getting away with not having to do a stand-in, but NOW at the worst time she was needed to go on stage. She finished dressing. Just before she went out on stage she peeped out into the crowd toward where she saw him last. The place was really getting crowded. But she couldn't find him. Maybe he left. She decided to hold on to that thought and do what she had to do.

There were no announcements of change dancers. Girls just went out and did their thing and at the end of the song or songs collected tips and came off stage. Tess knew there was a song that would work for her, so she rushed over to the music machine and pulled it up herself. With little time to spare, the music intro started, giving her enough time to take a deep breath. "Que será será," she mumbled to herself and stepped onto the stage and into the light.

She had wrapped herself, head to toe, with all the sheer fabrics she could find in the back room. On her head, around her hips, tied to each ankle and wrist, and a lot more places. It would take at least two songs to get through all of them. One piece covered her face right under her nose and mouth; the audience could only see her eyes. Tess did a dance walk around and removed one veil and cascaded it to the floor in front of her. The music was slow and melodic to start off, but there were many different tempo changes within the same song, and she needed that.

She knew the song well enough to put something together that really helped her. A pause came in the music, and at that same time Tess gracefully went down on both knees and reached for the ends of two smaller pieces of fabric. The music started again a little faster as she reached outward with the veils in hand, staying on her knees and swaying to the beat. Twirling them around and letting them flutter up into the air and cascade down. A graceful turning rise to a stand, she circled her hips side to side. The music picked up faster. A shoulder shimmy brought a wave of hollers from the audience.

Completely enthralled in the music, Tess turned her back to the audience and went into a shoulder shimmy backbend, grabbing the next veil and letting it go, and letting any tension she had go with it. Her hips went BUMP, BUMP, and circle, circle, BUMP, BUMP, circle, circle, pause, BUMP. With the last bump of her hips, she was down to only one large veil and the face-covering veils and her bra and harem pants, which were very sheer. She turned the veil into an envelope move she learned on one of the DVDs and shimmied until the end of the song. Through the veil she could see that all eyes were on her. And she felt that it was a different mood from the other dancers. This was liberating! With a whole lot of fun mixed in. A little creativity and mystery with the veils, very stimulating indeed. Then she remembered about him. She had let herself almost totally forget about him watching her dance!

With a few more beats to go, she tossed her hair in a circle, still wearing the veil on her face, and went down to the floor as the spotlight went off as planned for that song. Tess hurried to gather her tips and rushed off the stage as the crowd went wild for more. The other dancers had stopped what they were doing and were watching her short but different kind of dance. One dancer stopped Tess's quick escape and said, "Girl that was off the chain! You gonna teach us that dance, I know, right?!"

All Tess could say was "I didn't know I could." There was amazement in her eyes and a smile from ear to ear.

"You didn't look like it was your first time to me. You dropped it like it was SUPPOSED to be dropped! Classy, girl, definitely classy," the dancer added and took the stage.

"Now can you back that up?" Her boss's voice came out from around the corner.

He had watched her dance and had been waiting to talk to Tess. Tess spun around in surprise.

"Did your boyfriend see you?" He had gathered from watching her peek into the audience the whole time she was out on the stage, and only in a certain area of the club.

"What?" Tesseanna was surprised by his question, but quickly figured out how he could have come to his conclusion. "I don't know, but I will find out later, I guess," she answered with her face dropping the smile. She knew that either he saw her or his friends would tell him, if they recognized her.

"Anyway, the crowd loved your dance. What are you going to do next time?" Mr. Hamilton asked again. He had the look of money signs dancing in his eyes.

Tess in shock just shrugged her shoulders in answer to the question. She hadn't taken off all her clothes, and the crowd didn't seem to mind at all considering it was a strip club. She felt more like an artist than a stripper. She didn't have to go back on stage for the rest of the night and was glad about that.

The next day she looked for another prop to use just in case she had another surprise show to do. Going online again she found finger cymbals called "zills." That would take a little practice but it was doable. Zills were easy to rush order and once they arrived she found that they reminded her of basically snapping her fingers. Although she found that she needed to work different muscles of her fingers.

The finger cymbals she found to be energizing to work with. Her boss would be expecting a performance from her at any given time. He offered to pay her more to step in when needed. Tesseanna had no idea it would be like this. All she wanted was to be in the background waiting tables, not dancing.

She remembered the skirt she found for the date. That would make a nice, classy costume... *Oh! Rick! Our date! Tonight!*

She had totally forgotten about the date but not about his eyes. Nor had she forgotten about his broad shoulders and deep sultry voice. "Mmmmm, he sho is fine." Thoughts about his bright white smile made her smile with a girlish blush. She had to pull herself together, snap out of it, and rush to get ready on time. Although she wasn't thrilled with the arrangement, she agreed to meet Rick outside of the library anyway. He suggested meeting there since it was midway for both of them, and then going together from there.

She did her hair up in a genie ponytail while she was in the car for a playful, pulled-together look. She took the freeway, Interstate 94, that's the fastest way to travel in the Twin Cities, getting from downtown St. Paul to downtown Minneapolis. Traffic might be an issue tonight.

And it was. Something was going on downtown Minneapolis and had the freeway backed up for miles. Tess took the closest exit she could to the campus and did the stop and go all the way on side streets to the library.

Waiting for the light to change she noticed a restaurant that featured belly dancing. "Free lessons" also caught her eye on the sign.

"That sounds like a place I just might have to check out, at a later date for sure." She made a mental note of the location. Tess knew that she could learn a few new moves and get some formal training in what was now beginning to be her favorite dance.

Tesseanna saw Rick pacing around when she turned the corner to the library, and blew a short burst of her car horn.

He looked up and waved to acknowledge her.

Rick was a little preoccupied wrestling with a dilemma that he didn't want to share with anyone. He had plans for Tesseanna. She was to be the whipped cream and cherry of his upcoming talent show.

He needed something different and fresh to give him the upper hand at winning over some of his shareholders. No more hip hop or classical song and dance. The stockholders wanted something more and new to give up the money he needed for his venture. The biggest stockholder was his girl-friend's father. Rick needed the money and Tess was going to help him get it. All he had to do was convince Tesseanna to belly dance. He was already hooked up with one of his shareholders' daughters, but they weren't getting along too well lately; too bad she had no talent, and not much upstairs, just a rich daddy. Rick would have to keep this date low profile and appear professional. Slightly annoyed by her horn he waved to Tess.

"About time," he mumbled to himself while walking over to open the door for her after she parked her car.

"Hi, you made it!" he said, glancing at his watch.

"Sorry I'm a little late, traffic..." She was about to make an apology but stopped.

Oh, no he didn't just look at his watch. He was cute only without an attitude. She decided to let it slide and get a longer look into his personality, for now.

"I thought we would go somewhere different than the usual hangout spots," he said as he escorted her to his car and helped her in. "I always wanted to go to this restaurant but never got the chance, so I thought we would go there tonight, if you're up for it?" He smiled a dashing smile at her. How could Tess say no? "It looks like a nice little spot where we could talk," he continued.

Tesseanna couldn't help but smile and think, *He can be a good talker but can he be a good listener too?* He drove only a little while and stopped to park to her surprise, the restaurant that she had just passed on the way to meet him.

"The Polished Coins Restaurant?" Tess read out loud, sounding a little surprised.

"With belly dancing featured nightly. Have you been here before?"

"No, but I have passed by it." She started to wonder again if he had seen her or heard about her dancing on her job.

"Let's check it out together then!" Not waiting for her to agree or disagree, he jumped out of the car and opened the door for her. Showing off his best gentleman's chivalry and charm. Tess waited for him to open the door and she offered him her hand. To her delight he pulled her hand up to his lips and kissed it ever so softly. His mustache tickled and she couldn't help but giggle a schoolgirl's giggle. He tucked her hand around his waist and tucked his other hand around her waist. *What a nice tiny waistline she has*, he thought.

"You look great tonight," he whispered in her ear as they crossed the busy street and went in the door.

Lady was passing the entrance door and stopped when she saw the two new faces enter. She eyed Tess. She wondered for a moment if she knew her; she looked like a dancer or just in good shape.

"Can I seat you two for dinner this evening?" Lady asked the young couple, sensing that they had never been to her restaurant before. "Follow me," she instructed, not really waiting for a response. After they were seated Lady introduced herself, already planning for a surprise for later for the couple, Tess to be specific.

"I am Lady Amisi, the owner of this restaurant. I consider this to be an honor that you have chosen Polished Coins tonight. Welcome! I will be your hostess. I want you to have a joyous good time, so I would suggest to such a nice couple the sample platter. With this platter both of you can try a little of our most requested dishes. Would you like something from the bar to start?" After they put in their orders, taking Lady's suggestion, Lady excused herself.

Tesseanna marveled at the atmosphere of the restaurant. The curtains that hung stretched from ceiling to floor. Lighting was low enough for candles to be lit at every table, expensive-looking and exotic rugs underneath your feet at every step. The main glow was from the stage, which they were very close to.

Rick leaned over to her and locked eyes. "Have you ever seen belly dancing before?"

Tess didn't know what to say; she felt like a deer frozen in headlights. If she said she had, that might lead to many questions. He went on not really understanding her reaction, and assumed that she hadn't.

"It's a beautiful expression of dance," he continued, "not to mention the costumes they wear. You would look great in one. Maybe you should consider taking one of the classes that they offer here. I saw that they offer the first three classes free." He accented the "free" word to work in his favor.

Tess wondered where he was going with this. She could see that he had something in mind but what it was she wasn't quite sure. Maybe he wanted a personal show? Maybe he wanted her to perform in front of his friends. Did he see her that night at the club? Tess started to get a little on edge.

"Well…there is an opening in my talent show

that needs a little more diversity, a little more spice. Maybe an ethnic dance to feature talent." He reached over and touched her hand. "You definitely have the spice," he cooed.

"What!? You want me to dance, belly dance for you in your talent contest? Is that why you brought me here?" Tess's temper started to get hot, but remembering she was in a restaurant, she controlled herself. What kind of dance did he really want her to do? What did he see or hear about her? Did he see her dance at work that night?

If he did why didn't he just say so? Sensing a little uneasiness in her about the subject, he decided to talk about more of the artistic workings of his vision of the talent show. All while he was talking about other talents in the show Tess wanted to just ask him if he had been to the gentlemen's club where she worked. And what kind of girl he thought she was.

"Did I mention that there is a thousand-dollar cash prize awarded to the winner and a free one-year membership to the school?" Rick thought that might change her outlook on the matter.

Tesseanna had to give his request another thought after hearing that extra bit of info. She could use that money. And she would be around him more. "I won't say yes right now, but I will give it some thought and let you know soon, okay with you?" Tesseanna wanted to leave it at that for tonight. She felt she really didn't know him well enough to commit to anything right away. She tried to look into his soul, searching his eyes for his real reasons for his interest in her dancing.

"That sounds fair enough for me." Rick nodded and returned the gaze, searching for an idea of what her answer might be. He found her eyes to be mesmerizing. Her big, beautiful chestnut brown eyes with the dance of candlelight inside, her hair so sexy upswept, her lips with a soft hint of yummy.

"Your drinks," the waitress interrupted.

He pulled himself together, trying not to lead himself on. *Don't forget you're on a mission, and there is too much at stake to get involved*, he scolded himself. The school he now worked for could be his. If he played his cards just right.

The talent show would be his upstart and put his name on top. Right now it was in his girlfriend's daddy's name until it reached an earnings mark; then it became his, holding 60 percent of the stock with no strings attached. For now he had to stay focused. But what a lovely thing to stay focused on. Tesseanna.

The setting in the club was mostly lit with

candlelight but she seemed to glow from within. He felt that he wanted to tell her everything. Tesseanna had that effect on him. But he knew he couldn't do that, not now — he was too close to his dream. Maybe it could be their dream together, maybe someday.

Being a student of the body, physical therapy, she had studied body language. He was holding something back from her. Tesseanna couldn't take it anymore; she was just going to tell him what her temporary job was. She drew her breath. Just then their dinner came. That saved her, for now.

Their focus turned to the different foods of the sampler platter that Lady had suggested. The aroma of the food was spicylicious, a new word. He wanted to try her food and she wanted to try his food. The coffee was way too strong for her, so she kept drinking the sweet drinks from the bar. Their laughter seemed infectious all around them. They were getting to know each other. Getting comfortable, relaxing, and enjoying each other a little more.

"What a beautiful smile you have," he confessed, feeling like he had taken a truth serum. As they finished sampling their food and enjoying each other's company, another round of drinks came. He hadn't ordered any more drinks. A few minutes later Lady stopped by the table.

"This is a small thank you for being such a lovely couple. I hope you will enjoy the show, which will start soon." Lady made her exit, heading for the stage.

She had sent them the drinks, making sure that they stayed right where they were. If she needed her later and she knew she might. If things would only work out the way she planned. The drummers started to play.

A few moments later, Lady appeared off to the side of the stage. She introduced herself and welcomed everyone to The Polished Coins. Then she announced the first dancers. The curtains went up and all eyes were on the veiled dancers. They started the same way Tesseanna did on her job that night of her surprise dance. You couldn't see the dancers' faces until they unwrapped from the veil. Unlike Tess's many-veiled costume, the dancers used one large veil. Tess had seen and tried wrapping up in the veil before and had planned on using that move if she had to at work. Tess concentrated on one of the four dancers to learn from. She watched in enthusiasm, entranced by the choreography. The audience was also enjoying the dancers. Whoops and quite a few "Yeee-haas" as well as the rhythmic beat of hands showed they were enjoying every hip bump and shimmy that came in between the veil cascades. The veils' silky waves changed direction with the flip of the wrist.

Tess took mental notes of every move. The drummers were very expressive, even though one girl seemed to be in love with a drummer, you could see the love in their eyes across the the room. On what she thought to be the last dance of the show, the dancer did a drum solo that started out with the veil; she did a couple of hip accents and hip bumps that accented the music beats. In one dramatic move she enveloped herself inside the veil and then rested the veil on top of her head and peeked out through an opening. With a head slide, back and forth in a gliding motion.

"OH! That was sweet! I could do that!" Tess said that accidentally out loud and clear in her excitement. Out of the corner of her eye, she could see that he was watching her. She blushed.

12

Funesta

"I'm sooo sorry!" Funesta said, already at his side trying to help him up.

"What happened?" Afton said, still a little dazed. Funesta helped him off the floor and onto a chair near the door.

"I was practicing my cane exercises when you opened the door; you surprised me, and the cane slipped out of my hand, hit you in the head, and almost knocked you out. Your head is bleeding. We should get you to a doctor." She started to panic.

"We had children and…" he said, staring into her eyes. Just then the kids looking for their escaped cat ran by again.

"What?" Fun was wondering if he was delusional from the bump on the head.

"I mean… I'm okay." He pulled himself together. "My name is Afton. I'm sorry I startled you but you left your keys in the lock." He handed her the keys.

"Thank you! My name is Funesta. And I am

sorry to have cracked your head open with my cane!" They both laughed but his laugh was cut short by the pain in his head. They both noticed that she was still holding his arm, so she slowly let go.

"I hope I don't stop you from practicing. Are you a professional belly dancer?" Afton questioned.

"No, I just started taking lessons," she said as she went for a wet towel to place on his head. He flinched a little when she put the towel on the bump that was growing fast. He managed to stand up and walk over to the cane that was still on the floor. Fun caught herself checking out his broad shoulders, tight waist, big frame, and all so well-groomed look. He picked up the cane and handed it to her.

What was she saying? Oh yeah.

"My company makes these and I was just testing it out," she said.

Afton didn't want her to know that he had been watching her dance for a while. "I hope I can see you…dance…with the cane sometime," he stuttered.

"Maybe some other time." Funesta smiled.

He wanted to know more about the woman in his vision.

"I'm new to this area. Maybe you could show

me around? Maybe get a bite to eat?" he added, not letting her off the hook when he felt her hesitate. "I need a little something to keep up my strength after such a blow to the head." He smiled.

Ooh, what a smile, Funesta thought as she smiled too. "Okay, you're right. To keep up your strength, I'll take you out to get something to eat." Funesta didn't mind getting backed into a corner this time.

"Please, my treat indeed." Afton bowed. "I will meet you in the lobby in about an hour and a half, six o'clock, okay?"

Funesta noted the time.

"Six o'clock will be just perfect. See you then." Funesta left to get ready.

Afton watched Funesta go down the hall with her cane and CD player and he realized that he didn't get her phone number or apartment number. He would just trust that she wouldn't stand him up. But now was time for some pain pills!

It was a beautiful Saturday night. Funesta pondered where should they go to eat while she showered and got dressed. Then she remembered that she said she would come back to the Polished Coins that night. "I can't cancel on him after what happened and he will be waiting for me here in my own building right downstairs." She canceled that thought. *Maybe we will stop there later tonight for dessert or coffee and watch the show. He did say he wanted to see my cane dancing. We will see how the night goes.*

Afton was waiting for her with a flower in hand and a knot on his forehead, just a little black and blue. Still he looked good in a casual shirt and sport coat and jeans fitting just right. They matched colors both in a light turquoise with jeans, her in a denim short skirt, almost like they read each other's minds.

"I will drive you wherever you want to go." He took her hand and tucked it under his arm and escorted her to his car.

"Wow! That is the sharpest detailing on a car I have ever seen in my life, it's beautiful! Where did you have it done?" Funesta asked.

"Thank you, I did this one myself, which is the type of work I do." The red SUV was a true lipstick red in the front grill and gradient tinted to a purple plum to the back bumper, turning a common car into a piece of artwork, topped off with a glass shine.

"That's what brings me to Minnesota to start my own company called Car Fades. I think it should really…take off…get it, take off!" They both laughed at that silly joke as they took off down the street toward the downtown Minneapolis area for dinner.

"Where do you suggest we go?" Afton asked, trying not to let her see him check out her legs ever so slightly crossed in the car and watch the road at the same time!

"Well, there are a lot of nice places to go in the downtown area. What do you have a taste for?" Funesta said.

He eyed her for a moment, thinking, *Those lips would be a nice start*.

"Somewhere we could eat and talk, and I think I could be comfortable wherever you pick."

Funesta liked that Afton was not overbearing and was willing to compromise. Once in a bar and grill she had been before, they picked a nice cozy but not too private eating area to sit. They ordered right away; he knew what he wanted and so did she. Their table was right next to a beautiful scenic window view of the downtown area.

"Now tell me about yourself," Afton inquired. "Are you a native Minnesotan?"

Funesta didn't want him to move too fast; he was very smooth with his game, but it definitely was a game she wanted to play.

"Yes. Born and raised in St. Paul, with all the cold weather that I do not particularly like but

I'm still here." She smiled. "I finished school and found a job right out of college travelling to different states but still working on my master's. Now I work for a company that makes medical rehabilitation or physical therapy equipment. My department handles canes. That bump on your head is a sample of the quality workmanship we do. And by the way, that bump looks a lot better than it did." They both laughed again. He tried to ignore the slight throb on his temple. "Again, I am so sorry for that."

"That's okay, it's fine, really. My question is how can belly dancing canes be used for physical therapy?" Afton asked.

"An Middle Eastern restaurant that features bellydancing placed a order for a special order canes. Much different than what we sell normally. To get the canes to them on time, I had to hand deliver them myself. And I really got caught up in the fun!" she said, shimmying in her seat. Afton suggested to her surprise that they go to the Polished Coins for dessert.

Well, that was easy, Funesta thought. She was having a nice time with Afton, not like some of the other dates she had been on.

Fun felt as if she did not have to pretend. He was easy to talk to and easy to look at. His eyes sparkled when he talked about his new venture. Intelligent. He was a gentleman, using good etiquette and chivalry, opening doors, pulling out chairs… *Okay, what's wrong with him? Why isn't he taken yet? There is no tan marking or imprint on his ring finger and he can't be gay. Nope, he has checked out my legs and booty way too much for that. His feet and hands are a nice size. I will have to slow dance with him later to check that out.* One other thought came to mind. Afton might be like her, always moving around, not ready to settle down in one place. *I think he's a nice enough guy, so why isn't he taken?* Only one way to find out. After the two finished eating, they headed to the Polished Coins.

Lady Amisi was seating guests and chitchatting with everyone as she worked her way around the room. She always kept an eye on the door. Like she kept an eye on every little thing going on in her restaurant/club. Relief came over her when Lady saw her fast learner Funesta enter the club, just as she promised, and with a handsome gentleman friend too. Lady had found out just a bit earlier that she was going to be more than a couple of dancers short due to the flu. And she also knew that Funesta could be an impromptu fill-in dancer if need be. Lady had one other in mind as an extra dancer. A plan started to take shape, but she may need a couple of more dancers for this plan to work out right.

Fun had taken the rest of the weekend off, so she had started to relax a little; a dessert and something to drink was just what she needed. They had just finished ordering when Lady came to their table.

"Funesta, you made it!" Lady hugged her. "I am so glad you came tonight. I believe tonight will be a night that you won't forget. What a handsome young man." Lady reached for Afton's hand. Fun introduced them.

"Lady Amisi, this is Afton, a new friend of mine, and yes, he is a knockout even with a bump on his head." They both laughed, and Fun went on to tell Lady about how he got that bump, and Lady laughed too.

"Funesta has shown me the beautiful canes that her company has made for your company, close up. I have never seen a cane dance in belly dancing before." Afton touched the almost forgotten bump on his head.

"Tonight you will see them in action, again, but not so close!" Lady teased Afton. "But now your desserts are here! I hope to see you later tonight at the after party as my welcomed guests.

The show should start in a few minutes, enjoy!" She was gone.

"A knockout, huh!" he said to Fun.

She found herself blushing in his gaze. She tried the dessert. "Ooooh, this is delicious! Try this!" She was happy to have changed the focus.

He tried her dessert and added, "Now try mine!" He tempted her with a sample of his dessert. He couldn't keep his eyes off of her—so strong yet feminine, intelligent and fun. Why wasn't she taken? Well, he wasn't going to let this lady get away, no way! Besides, he had seen their future together and he liked it. So he decided to go for it.

"Do you have a boyfriend?" He held his breath for the answer.

She shook her head. "Nope."

"Well, I can't say I'm sorry to hear that. Maybe we could see more of the town together," he said, trying not to seem desperate.

When she said, "I'd like that," it was music to his ears!

Fun was shocked to hear herself. *How did that just come out of my mouth like that?* Her mind said one thing but her heart spoke for her. She felt herself relax even more.

The drummers started to warm up and she

noticed a young girl walking over to them. She wondered if they were dating or something by the look on their faces. *This should be an interesting night,* she thought. When she looked over at Afton, he had a sparkle in his eyes. Maybe it was just the candlelit tables or was it something else? She felt a blush come over her, starting at her toes and working its way up…

"Good evening ladies and gentlemen." Her thoughts were interrupted by Lady's greeting. "Welcome to the Polished Coins." Anything after that was sort of blended into the background noise for the two lovebirds. Only after the first dancer stepped onto the stage did Fun notice what was going on around them. The dancer with the veil. Fun took note of all the big gestures. She knew some of the moves from the classes. She felt herself mimicking some of the moves in her seat, but she didn't want him to see her doing so. It wasn't like her to be shy. The second dancer's costume was so beautiful. "I LOVE that outfit!" she said out loud with a passion.

"Yeah, you would look good in that," he said.

Fun just smiled at him and said, "It must be very expensive. Look at all that beading!"

Their third dance was the liveliest dance she saw. The beading in black and white had a matching arm, ankle, and headpiece. The long strands of bugle beads came down to her belly button at a point from her bra. The skirt had the same pattern of beads to match draped over her hips and over the high splitting skirt. The beads emphasized each movement from shoulder shimmies to hip bumps with sparkling waves of movement. The drummers' outfits were not as colorful, more of a casual comfort look in tunics with some in long vests. Funesta was disappointed that there wasn't a longer cane dance featured tonight; only one dancer had a short cane dance, but she also noticed that there were fewer dancers than before. But it was a lovely show. The company was a whole lot better this time, no offense to Lady. Funesta and Afton continued to taste each other's desserts.

13

Seri

"Seri, baby, are you all right?" Again not waiting for an answer, Thomas leaned down to her and kissed her like it was the first kiss and the last kiss. A passionate kiss, an "I love you" kiss, "I missed you" kiss all in one. "I was soooo scared I lost you," he managed to say after a deep breath. She could hear the fear in his voice as he spoke, but she still felt the kiss he left on her lips more than anything he was saying. Something that she hadn't felt in a long time. Some of the weakness left and a different kind of feeling came, almost making her want to jump up out of the bed or bring him into it. Just then their two daughters came rushing into the room.

"Mom, you're awake!" they both exclaimed and took their mother's side. After hugs and kisses all around Seri asked how they had gotten there so quickly.

"Mom," the oldest said, "you had a heart attack, and you have been out for about three days!"

The youngest answered, "We put things on

hold without a second thought for you, and you know that."

"WHAT! A heart attack! And three days I've been in here!" Seri almost rose out of the bed with that news. She felt like Rip Van Winkle waking up from a long slumber, with no beard.

"The doctor gave you something to help you sleep and to bring down your blood pressure; you needed to rest. When I was coming down the stairs I heard the fall. You must have hit the floor real hard."

"That would explain the cut and headache," Seri said, feeling the cut on her head.

"The cut probably came when the barbeque glass jar broke; I think you were going for the aspirin bottle in the cabinet on the other side of the kitchen."

"Yes, I was. I also remember you calling me when I was in the ambulance."

"Oh yeah! I probably made a fool of myself that night. I was so scared that I had not told you everything I wanted to tell you. I thought I had lost you. You had started to stabilize in the ambulance when all of a sudden you took a turn for the worse! I didn't know what to do; all I knew was that I wanted to be with you. You were in serious condition for too long. I did perform a little

CPR on you waiting for the paramedics to come. Just what you taught me and the girls. They said if I hadn't, you wouldn't have had a chance. But I know you. You are a fighter and you would have made it though. And you would have kicked my butt or haunted me the rest of my natural born days if I had messed that up." He smiled.

Seri was released two days later from the hospital with a new outlook on life and relationship with her husband and daughters. To take better care of herself became a high priority. She had lost a little weight while she was in the hospital to start off on the right foot, but she needed to lose a little more. Her diet was closely monitored during her stay in the hospital, but now it was up to her to eat fresh fruits, vegetables, and oats for good fiber every day. Working out at least a half an hour a day was approved and recommended by her doctor as an additional three times a week regimen. The workout had to be low impact, nothing too harsh on her joints, bones, or heart. Her husband had an uphill climber in his man cave, where he worked out often to keep that fifty-five year young body looking good.

She started with that at first. That didn't last long. It was too boring. Even doing it while watching television did nothing to keep her wanting to work out on it. But she found herself ordering alternative cardio workouts from infomercials on the TV. Nothing held her interest for long. Seri wanted to improve her upper body and her bootylicious lower body with special attention on the waistline. Whatever it was, it had to be fun. Something she would look forward to every day. Otherwise, it would just collect dust like the rest of her workout toys. When she went online to see what her options were, one thing stood out for her and that was dancing.

When she and her husband were younger they used to go to the clubs to dance. Now of course the music had changed and they really weren't into rap music. Most of the clubs were catering to a younger crowd. It had been a long time since they went out just to dance. Other dances she found online like Latin dancing were spicy. That was nice. Two-stepping was okay. Ballroom and pole dancing, "Nope, not for me." She moved on. Belly dancing? She found many DVDs for beginners for that type of dance. She liked the moves and the costumes as she watched some of the video trailers on the computer. This was something she could do in her own house, by herself.

"Yes, working the areas that I want to slim down directly. That sounds perfect and a little sexy." She decided to keep it to herself and not show it to her husband until she got better at it. Possibly he might have the pleasure of a surprise private show someday. She smiled at the thought and ordered the DVDs next day shipping. The next day when her package came her husband was not expected home for two or three hours, a perfect time to try the disks out with nobody home to see her look crazy.

First she went into her closet to find a suitable hip scarf. The closet was extremely full, but she found one of many scarves in her possession. This particular one was a beautiful sheer pink with long, flowing fringes all around the whole scarf. This would be the first time she wore it. It was bought during a "mad at my husband" shopping spree. After tying the scarf around her hips, she decided which disk to play first—the veil or the drum solo? At first she felt a little silly, not graceful like the teachers she was watching. But the more she practiced the moves and choreography, the better she became. She was always a quick study. Like all the other workouts, she always tried to finish before her husband came home. The workouts that she found were indeed low impact, so her knees didn't hurt, but it was upbeat enough to keep her heart rate up to burn calories and help bring down her blood pressure, along with eating right.

At first she felt sort of silly, so she stopped and made sure her husband wasn't home yet. Keeping an eye on the clock, and the window, she guessed she had at least a half an hour before he was due home so she continued. By the time he made it home Seri had just finished the stretching in the cool-down part of the workout. All her muscles she never knew she had needed a good stretch.

After work the next day she stopped by the bookstore to see if there was anything else on DVD she could buy. There were quite a few to pick from. She couldn't decide on one or two, so she took one of each. Then Seri hurried home before her husband got home to try a couple more out. The DVDs didn't disappoint. There were shim-mies upon shimmies to burn off the fat. "No pain, no gain," Seri said out loud, trying to stay moti-vated and upbeat, even with the burn that signals the burning of calories. The instructors were very easy to follow and gave good advice.

Shimmies are just moving your knees back and forth at different speeds. If you find that your shimmy gets out of control and stiffens up on you, slow down to a steady beat to regain con-trol. Then bring it back up to medium pace to a full shimmy timing. Seri shimmied, forming the shape of a figure eight on the floor. Seri followed the advice about slowing down when her shimmy almost stopped at certain points and keeping it up until the shimmy gets stronger. But that was just the Egyptian shimmy; there were more shimmies to try for the lower body toning. Shoulder accents and alternating snake arms worked her upper body. She was so into her workout that she didn't notice the time. Seri had no idea that her husband had come home and had been watching her for some time. He was really enjoying the show. He had forgotten that she liked to dance when they first met.

"I can't let this moment get away," He whispered to himself as he pulled out his camera phone and started to record her dancing. He knew if she saw him she would stop, and he wanted to get as much as he could of her.

Seri took on her shimmies with power. Since she had curvaceous hips and a whittling down waistline, the drum solo easily became her favorite part of dancing. Never before had she liked her full hips. All of her clothing showed that by covering them up. Shaking them with a scarf on top drew attention to that area. "Shimmy, shimmy, shimmy. POP! Bye, bye, cholesterol and high blood pressure; hello, tiny waist and tight thighs." She liked the way working out made her feel—strong, powerful, and in control. She wasn't going to let a weak heart get the best of her; it was just going to have get stronger too. Seri kept her workout secret from her family. All they knew was that she was losing weight, by eating healthy. All her clothes were getting a little sloppy on her new smaller size.

"Time to go shopping," her daughters told her on a zoom call. No need to tell her twice. Any reason to go to the largest mall in America is a good reason. And lucky for her it wasn't far away. No more plus sizes for her; she would have to shop in some different stores now, and the Mall of America had it all! She knew MOA well.

On the way to the mall she caught a glimpse of a restaurant billboard ad. She went by too fast to read everything but she did catch "BELLY DANCE, Free Trial" and she sort of knew where the address was.

"Well alrighty then," she said to herself. "I'll just check this out quickly and then get all up into the shopping experience that I sooo need right now." It was very easy to find a parking spot since it was right on the bus line. *Polished Coins, well, this sounds like fun*. And she went in. The restaurant was surprisingly busy even though there were only a couple of cars in the parking lot. A beautiful woman came up to her and asked her if she would like a table. Seri almost didn't hear her because she was overwhelmed by the lavish décor of the restaurant.

"Ah, no, not right now, but could you tell me how to register for the free trial belly dance class?"

"Yes, I can. I will be your teacher. Is this for the advanced class?" Lady eyed her with a hopeful glance.

"No, sort of a beginner." Seri didn't know if it was good or bad to have been self-taught by DVDs or not. All she had was a mirror to tell if she had been doing the moves correctly or not and just by her own standards.

"All right, we can work with that, even though I think you may be holding back!" Lady signed her up for the next class to start that weekend. Lady Luck was smiling on Lady Amisi. All Seri needed to bring was a hip scarf. Barefoot is recommended to belly dance and/or one well-fitted sock to help you spin on the floor.

After she signed up for classes, Seri headed for the Mall of America. So many new stores for her to shop in her new size. First she stopped at one of her favorite stores to pamper herself in. An all-natural, cocoa butter infused with glitter. It made her skin sparkle when she wore it as a base. Also bath bombs to make her skin soft for a long, soothing soak in the tub was always a special treat. There were also bath bombs couples could use together; that sounded like fun too. She bought one of those just in case. Then it was off to find just a couple of outfits for her new shapely size to start off with. Something to show off her smaller waistline. The basics were a good starting spot. Black and white with a pop of color would be a more age-appropriate attire. *That's nice but I also need something a little more fun*, she thought. In one of the carts in the west market she found a vendor that had the most beautiful scarves she had ever seen. The ones with fringes work the best for the shakings of a shimmy. "I could add coins later if need be." She added a couple of those to her collection. Browsing around the west court she also found a specialty store with hair jewelry. She didn't think she needed it because she already bought all her hair supplies at Earth's Beauty Supply in St. Paul, but a little more bling is always more fun, and also to change up her look.

And on a different level of the mall (There are three levels of shopping stores in the Mall of America, Minnesota. The fourth floor has the clubs and movie theater, just saying.), Seri found some comfortable workout wear so she could move without restriction. Cotton with a nice blend of spandex intertwined in the material to breathe and stretch when needed. And of course she couldn't leave without a tasty treat! So many to pick from in any direction; north court and south court had the most sections just packed with food choices. Remembering to eat healthy, heart healthy, all the time narrowed the choices down some, but not much. Healthy should have mostly vegetables, and steamed at that. She had a hard time picking. Seri chose a salad, with the dressing on the side. And for dessert, frozen yogurt with the works on top!

When Seri arrived home with all her shopping finds, she found a few messages on her cell phone and home phone. She had forgotten to take her cell phone with her; it was still sitting on the charger. The messages were from her daughters and husband wondering where she was and to call if she needed anything. Seri had told her husband that she was going shopping at the mall, so he knew that might take a while. She called them all back and everyone was now relaxed about her whereabouts, and health. Tom, her husband, wouldn't be home for another two hours.

"Time for some self-pampering," Seri joyfully said out loud. She ran a bath with the bath bomb she just purchased at the mall. Flameless, scented candles gave her a peaceful retreat. After a half hour or so, the phone woke her up asleep in the tub. It was her husband.

"Get dressed. I want to take you out somewhere special tonight," Tom said, sounding excited and suspicious.

"Where are we going?"

"To a restaurant you might enjoy," he said with a boyish excitement in his voice she hadn't heard for a long time that really piqued her curiosity.

"Okay, heels or flats?" she asked.

"Flats, but not too flat," he answered, knowing that old question was her way to find out if they were going dancing or not.

It must be oldies night somewhere, she thought. Another surprise was that he also requested her "fly" skirt. He called it that because it fit well in the waist and hips but just like a gored skirt it had a lot of twirl and movement to it when she danced.

"Go wan now and get yourself ready. I'll be there in about an hour and a half," Tom said with a fake Southern accent. They hadn't gone out dancing in years, maybe at a wedding or something but not just because. What was he up to? Well, it sounded like fun whatever it was. She hurried to her closet and found the skirt he requested. In the mirror she made a couple of spins in the skirt, which to her surprise went very well with the scarf or hip scarf she bought at the mall. After a few more hip bumps and horizontal figure eights that she learned to do with flowing arm cascades, she felt as if she was a dancer out on the stage. When she looked up at the clock on the wall out of the corner of her eye, she saw a head pop back out of sight!

"How long have you been watching me, you Peeping Tom!" She'd know that head anywhere.

"Caught me!" Her Peeping Tom came into their bedroom from his hiding spot. He grabbed her around the waist and kissed her long and hard. When he came up for air he looked into her eyes and kissed her again, and his hands cupped her curvy butt. She felt again the heat and passion like when they first met. That hadn't happened in a long time.

"We better get going before it gets too late," Tom said, bouncing his dark eyebrows and smiling. When they got themselves ready, zipping up her back zipper with a neck-nuzzling kiss, he went into the living room and she followed.

"I almost forgot... I have a little something for

you." He turned and picked up a small box and handed it to her. She almost dropped it. Not sure if it was because of the surprise of getting a present from him or that she was still tingling from the kissing.

"Something lovely for my lovely," Tom said in a sexy whisper. She opened the box with a surprised giddiness. Inside the box was a fresh flower necklace. This was something that she had never seen before, anywhere! The three flower stems were encased in a small glass bubble that had a small amount of water in them to keep the flowers fresh. The flower matched her floral skirt that he had requested she wear tonight. Seri was speechless only for a moment. Sensing that she liked it, he helped her put it on her neck and fastened it in the back. She finally spoke. "This is luscious."

"Yeah, you are," he said in a sexier voice. "We'd better get going before we are late."

"You did make reservations," she said gleefully.

"Maybe," he mused, being mysterious. In the car he had a blindfold for her. He didn't want to give her any idea where they were heading. He still had more surprises to unfold in store for her. He was not totally sure how his wife would react if she knew what he had planned earlier for her that day. What he had done?

Only when she stepped through the front door would he take the blindfold off. The rest would unveil before her eyes. So excited and a little nervous he pulled up in front of the restaurant. Seri was enjoying the mystery and spontaneity of her husband; she could also feel his nervousness.

Being married for over thirty years had that side effect on each other. Since her fall in the kitchen, he had been just like when they were first dating. Most or all of the fighting had disappeared. Normally she was a control freak and not really into surprises, but she could get used to this new attitude and longitude now that she was home from the hospital. When the car stopped she was about to take off the blindfold but he stopped her.

"Not yet, let me get your door first." Tom came around the car and helped her out of the car and across the street arm in arm. Seri was still blindfolded — that was a lot of trust — and she could hear that it was a busy street. He opened the door, and they went into the restaurant with her holding tightly to his arm.

"Now can I look?" Seri pleaded.

"Okay, okay, yes, dear, you can take off the…"

Before he could finish his sentence, Seri had snatched the blindfold off her face so fast that she nearly took out her eye with her manicured gel nails.

"Where are we? This place is beautiful." All around were cascading window treatments and candlelit tables. She recognized it but was still in shock to be there at night when the atmosphere had changed from the day.

"Welcome to the Polished Coins," came a voice from the crowd. "I can seat you now. Please follow me." Lady was waiting for them to arrive. Her graceful silhouette emerged from out of the soothing darkness. Seri recognized Lady Amisi but said nothing; she just smiled and followed her to their table. "Oooooo, you did make reservations!" Seri exclaimed. She also noticed that they had one of the best seats in the place next to the stage.

"I wanted to take you somewhere different and special tonight." He paused. "I have a confession to make…"

HUH oh! Here we go, here comes the bomb! "Come on, drop it on me. I knew it was too good to be true!" she exploded.

"Wait, it's not like that, woman!" he hissed, trying to keep his voice down.

She carried on. "Fancy, nice place, passionate kissing getting me all excited, and all the hush,

hush. Let me get my drink on first." She finally sat back.

"For real, it ain't like that! But let us get our drink on first anyway," Tom said calmly. "What would you like?"

"You know what I want."

"As you wish!" He waved to the waitress. The drinks were brought in an instant. "I took the liberty of ordering for you, my fineness." He nodded and plates of food arrived at the table. "This is a sampling of the menu, with low sodium," he added. "Now, what I was *trying* to say is that I have been watching you dance for a while now, and I think you are very good and..." He couldn't finish the rest of his sentence.

"What! You Peeping Tom!" Seri put her hands on her hips, happy that it wasn't anything bad like what was running through her mind.

"I think you have gotten pretty good and I have been also taping you and I showed the tape to our hostess Lady Amisi and she wants you to join her classes." He waited for a battle, almost squinting, ready for the fallout.

"You showed a video of me dancing, to her?" A quick flash of anger came over her, and then she asked it again with a calmer voice.

"Yes, you aren't mad at me, are you?" he said

with the old Southern accent he only used to soften her up when he thought he had done something wrong.

"What did she say? About my dancing?"

Surprised, he continued. "She has a place for you in her class on Saturdays in the advanced class. She also said that you have one of the strongest hip shimmies she has ever seen on someone who has never had any formal training. That sounds like you're a natural, baby!"

"Thank you, dear. I think I will take your advice and take lessons. This food looks delicious!" They toasted with their wineglasses and dug into their appetizer plate. He was relieved that Seri didn't take his head off, and proud of himself that she was going to take his advice. Not long after they had finished eating, the music started to play. Lady, their hostess, announced the first dancer and the troupe named Swaysa and the Swaying Gems! They were really good. Very engaging. So professional and polished. The costumes were beautiful and expensive-looking. Seri felt herself wanting to get up and join them dancing. She took in every move and stored it in memory to try out later. She had always been a fast learner, when it came to dancing or anything else. She thought that the dancers were very graceful compared to herself. Something Seri had already been working on in front of the bigger mirror she had just purchased for her workout room at home.

Seri LOVED the show. Her favorite was the drum solo of course because of the hip bumps and shimmying, and now she felt more confident that a professional had seen her work. Saturday would be very exciting, like a coming out, no longer hiding her dancing workout fun. Seri leaned over and gave her husband a couple of kisses to let him know she wasn't mad but actually happy. And a little turned on.

14

Start the Show!

After the first two performances ended, Lady took to the stage with her beauty and personality.

"Can I have your attention please?" Lady said, almost not needing a microphone with her command of the stage. A hush crossed the room like a wave.

"Let me introduce myself; my name is Lady Amisi," she said with a hand undulating and a curtsy. "Welcome to my restaurant. I hope you are enjoying this beautiful art form tonight. I have been dancing almost all my life, and teaching other women this expression of dance is simply a joy for me. With this type of dance the movement can be the same but is unique as the dancer dancing. Belly dance is for young and old, skinny or healthy." Lady grabbed her own butt and gave it a little shake and smiled. The crowd laughed. And she continued.

"Tonight we are going to do something special. As you might know I give free beginning lessons here at the top half of this restaurant on weekends. I would like to invite four lovely ladies up to the stage to enjoy a journey in belly dance." Lady's eyes gazed out into the audience.

"Please give a hand to SERI!" Lady signaled for Seri to come to the stage.

"What, ME! Go up there?" said a totally shocked Seri. Her husband jumped up and started whooping and cheering for her to go up to the stage. "Did you plan this?" Seri asked her husband as she stood.

"Well, maybe." He smiled.

She got up and stood next to Lady on stage, nervous but ready.

"Next may we have Shylessa joining us up here?" Lady added. "Lady Bird, I think there is a spot waiting for you in the drummer's area." She obviously had talked to Bird's new friend for information on the two ladies.

"Oh no, she didn't just call us to come up there!" Shy covered her mouth that she couldn't close in surprise. Bird, however, had jumped up and was on her way to her reserved place at the side of her new drummer friend. Lady gave Shy a little time to navigate through the crowd to get on stage.

"We're going to have a 'Fun' night tonight.

Funesta, please join us on stage. I'm sure your gentleman friend won't mind if we steal you away for a moment." Lady winked at the couple.

Not really surprised at all, Fun leaned over and whispered, "You got your wish." He smiled and clapped for her.

"I do need one more." Lady came down off the stage and walked right up to Tesseanna. "Such a beautiful lady, please join us." Tess tried to resist but Lady was not taking no for an answer; she took Tess's hand and guided her onto the stage and lined her up with the rest of the chosen ones.

15

Diamond Coins

"Ladies and gentlemen, after a short intermission the new troupe will perform a short dance for you that they have just learned. Please let's encourage them," Lady said and started the applause. The audience cheered and clapped as the ladies took a curtsy and Lady escorted them behind the stage curtains. The backstage area was extremely deceiving from the front view of the stage; it was really roomy and spacious. It hid a wide assortment of props from mirrors, trees, floating windows, and oversized doors. The hustle and bustle of dancers and stagehands weaving in and out of side doors added to the feeling of energy of the moment.

Backstage Lady was brought a large basket full of glittering, silky veils and held each one up to the faces of the ladies to see which color complemented them the best with their skin tone. Each hip scarf sparkled like diamonds, full of beads and golden or silver coins that made a wave of tinkling noise. While she did this, she sang a little ditty that went:

"Take your cues from me…easy as can be… Move a little, move a lot… Just enough to make it POP! I want to thank you all for participating in a beginners show tonight. I know a couple of you. Funesta, I'm sure you are ready for this," Lady Amisi said as she tied a hip scarf around Fun's hips.

"I'm not as sure as you are," Fun said, a little nervous.

"I could tell you were ready from the time you came backstage to the after party. You can teach the teacher something new." Lady smiled as she finished the hip scarf. Turning her attention to Seri with a smile, she said, "You, my lady, have a lot of power in those hips. Did your husband tell you that he thinks so too? Your lovely husband shared with me footage of you working out and I think you are incredible."

"Thank you, that means a lot. And yes, he told me some of what he has been up to. I thought I was working out only to burn off calories and cholesterol," Seri said nervously.

"For you, a beautiful five-tiered, noise-shaking hip scarf perfect for shimmying." Lady gave it to Seri to tie on herself; she knew she knew how.

"Shylessa, is that right?" Lady asked as she handed Shy a matching hip scarf and veil.

"Yes, ma'am." Shy tied the veil on her hips and gave a solo twirl of the veil around her head and brought it up in front of her to let the air catch it and let it fall gently down.

"Well, I see you speak veil." Lady happily took notice of how well she handled the veil. Lady turned to Tess. "I think I surprised you the most of all. What is your name please?"

Tess was a little hesitant with her response. She was not sure about dancing in front of a crowd, or him, considering what he just had asked of her minutes before about dancing for his production.

"Tesseanna," she answered in almost a whisper.

"Tesseanna, what a beautiful name. I think it fits you marvelously. I see in your eyes a little flirtiness, you and your boyfriend. This is your first date, am I right?" Lady asked.

"Yes, how did you know?" Tess asked with surprise.

"I can tell that you are trying to figure each other out. He might be holding something back. Some might say I have a sixth sense, but I don't want to pry into your business. Just be careful."

Lady continued gathering all the ladies around her.

"When you let your inner beauty shine,

dancing with happiness in your soul and your heart, that will transfer through to the whole audience. We will do just a few steps, nothing too complicated, simple and elegant. First, a figure eight with the hips." Lady demonstrated. "Sway your hips in the shape of an eight on the floor, at the count of four times. Now do it with me." They all followed directions.

"Perfect! Next a shoulder shimmy. Start slow, shoulders back and forth, then build up a little faster to the beat and walk in a circle while shoulder shimmying. Arms out proudly, hold the veils tight but not too tight. Fantastic!

"Now let us try a veil move that I call the whirlwind. Bring your veil to the front of you and swirl it from one side to your other side." Lady was not surprised by the flawless execution but by how quick they were learning. So she decided to add more to the routine than she planned.

"We will snake arm with the veil, adding a flip to the wrist, four times; follow your hand movement with your head and eyes, and smile. We are having fun. Then music will rest for a bit. And bring the veil up behind you, slowly for another four counts. Now we will repeat from the top and end with an eight-count hip shimmy and a pose with our veils released in the air above our heads to have a magical finish. Let's go through it one more time, but don't forget I will be dancing along with you, right off to the side. If you miss a step, you meant to do that ! Just pick back up and follow along, and your best will be perfect!" Lady added after the second go-through, "I am very proud of our new dance troupe."

The ladies all looked at each other. Shylessa, Tesseanna, Funesta, and Seri felt proud too; they joined hands in a circle and let out some of their nervousness with giggles and laughter.

"Now we are ready!" Lady said, overjoyed by how things were working out.

The drummers had started to play already, with their newest drummer, Lady Bird, doing very well keeping up with her newly learned drum and rhythm. There were a few dancers on stage with some other ladies and men from the audience dancing and having fun. Lady nodded to the drummers and they quickly ended the song and everyone exited the stage. The curtains came down on the outside stage; they were almost sheer, not heavy as the inside stage curtains so no one could see the new troupe move to the center of the stage. The audience knew what was next.

"Okay, ladies." Lady locked eyes with each. "You look like a beautiful belly dance troupe. You are here to have fun, so don't hold back, enjoy the movements, and mostly enjoy yourselves."

The crowd started clapping and cheering even before they saw the new dancers. Even Bird stopped drumming to get her camera ready to take pictures of her friend on stage, belly dancing—who would have thought it. The curtain went up. And there they were, sparkling in hip scarves, matching veils, and adrenaline-energized smiles. Seri's husband may have been the loudest cheerer in the crowd. His camera was on rapid shot and auto zoom. She gave him a little wink. He had gone to so much trouble and she wanted to make him proud. Tesseanna looked for her man and caught his eyes but he was on his cell phone. Who was he talking to at this hour? *And on our date!* That was a little rude. She could tell he was trying to end the call by his head nodding and the way he was acting. And he did end the call and finally stood up and clapped for her. Tess forced a smile his way, but she was just not feeling him anymore. Lady Amisi noticed also. Funesta could feel her date's eyes only on her. She purposely looked around at the rest of the audience before she looked his way because she knew she was already blushing. He blew her a kiss. She felt a little fire within her start to glow and grow. Her voice within said, "I think I'll keep him." She smiled at him. Shylessa didn't feel shy at all. A little nervous but not like she used to feel when she had a big Spirits praise dance piece at church to perform. It seemed different, no stress. Somehow she felt ready to dance. Her mother of course would have a major fit if she knew what her daughter was about to do right now. She quickly took that thought out of her mind to get back to happy thoughts. She gave Bird a big smile for the camera. Lady was off to the side so that they all could see her, but they had command of center stage. Just as practiced in four counts each.

The music started.

Figure eights, then small hip circle, then large hip circle Repeat. Shoulder shimmy in a walk around circle both directions.

Whirlwind for four counts.

Snake arms with wrist flips.

Repeat from the top.

Shimmy with power. 1.2.3.4.5.6.7. Veil up, release the veil and pose.

Before the veils even hit the floor, the audience was on their feet. They were having fun on the stage and everyone felt it. Not one misstep, which was unheard of for a new group of new dancers to achieve. A flawless dance. The audience and the other dancers, amazed that they learned so quickly, applauded approvingly. This was a brilliant idea Lady Amisi had, just because she was short on dancers because of the flu. Now she had a troupe!

"Ladies and gentlemen, these ladies are diamonds, am I right?" Lady outstretched her hand toward them to accept more applause and signaling the ladies to take a curtsy for the audience. Someone in the audience yelled out, "Diamond Coins!" and instantly the whole restaurant cheered and chanted, DIAMOND COINS, DIAMOND COINS, DIAMOND COINS.

"Well, I think we have a winning name for our new troupe," Lady concurred. "May I introduce you to The Diamond Coins! Let's see them individually, shall we?

"Shylessa, could you show us a veil move?" Lady nodded to the drummers who knew what to do, then nodded to Shy, who was taken by surprise and picked up her veil.

"Woohoo! Go, Shylessa! Do it, girl!" Bird couldn't contain her excitement for her friend. She was still playing with the drummers, only stopping here and there to take pictures and cheer her friend on. Shy pulled herself together, remembering what she learned on the DVDs. She made a four-point turn while closing herself inside the veil, making an envelope. She rested the top part of the veil on her head and hip shimmied while peeking out through the veil's opening. Shylessa finished the move off with a quick veil opening and posed, smiling, amazed and happy she pulled it off without chickening out. Bird was the loudest and jumped to her feet clapping, shocked at the openness of her normally shy friend.

"Wonderful! Next we have Tesseanna to show us how to shoulder shimmy!" Lady gestured for her to step forward because she sensed her hesitation.

The drummers layered a little faster tempo to their continuing beat for Tess to play with. Tess picked up on the change of tempo and threw caution to the wind. Interpreting the music with her shoulders, she started shoulder shimming and stepped out in front. She held the shimmy in the shoulder for a few beats and then sent the shimmy down to her hips and back up to her shoulders. She kept this movement going and decided to layer a level change onto her dance. Shoulder shimmy down and hip shimmy up, arms up, pose to finish. Tess felt energized with the roar of the crowd.

I could get used to that, Tesseanna thought while curtsying to the audience.

Meanwhile, Funesta could feel the butterflies in her stomach. She knew she was next. Lady handed her one of her own canes from what seemed to her to be from out of the air.

"We have a new student of mine here tonight, Funesta! Please show us a cane step you have been practicing." Lady also held her veil for her as she gave her the cane and took a bigger step back so as not to get hit with a flying cane. "Keep it simple and smooth," Lady whispered. Fun took a breath, and so did the audience it seemed. Afton felt the bump on his head and held his breath. The drum roll started. She started with a slow cane rotation for eight beats and switched to the other hand for eight beats. Totally concentrating on what she was doing, she became more confident and let go…of a smile.

"OOOhoo's" came from the crowd.

The cane twirled around her fingers; she had total control. She switched from hand to hand three more times with a two-count beat, then held onto the came with both hands in a three-point spin into a final cane up above the head, posing to fin-ish. The audience could feel the nervousness and uncertainty she had when she started her improv dance, and when she ended with confidence, that made her dance even more worthy of an ovation.

She breathed, curtsied, and took her place in the lineup still on the stage. Seri knew Lady was saving the hip bumps for her. She was ready. Seri had worked out to many different styles of drum solos, so she was comfortable with the changing drumbeat to more of a primal, earthy emotion in the drum solo.

Hips, don't fail me now, she thought.

"Now for a powerhouse beginner, Seri!" Lady cheered on.

Seri was ready and stepped forward with a hip down, down, up, down, up, down, down, up, down, up while the drummer played a classic beat called a maqsoum rhythm. Her arms alternated simultaneously in an L pattern, one arm above her head and one arm out to the side. Her husband Thomas of course was the loudest cheerer in the room when she turned her back to the crowd and repeated her hip bumps. With sharp energy in each of her hip movements, she looked over each of her shoulders at the audience for just the count of four and hip bumped around in a circle and returned facing forward. She increased the speed and intensity of her hip bumps, turning them into a coin-shaking, dynamic, full-on hip shimmy. Her head and her hands followed the movements of her hips like accents; she didn't forget to come up and around in a full circle with her hips while she shimmied, cascading arms down in beautiful circling hand flutters to add the right touch, then up with both hands to finish. A little out of breath but totally feeling wonderfully good, Seri looked out to a standing ovation. That felt exquisitely good. SERI!

"Let's hear it for our new troupe, Diamond Coins!" Lady boasted. "Thank you all for participating tonight and I am excited to see our new troupe next week for the start of free classes. You ladies can keep and bring the hip scarfs to any and all the classes. Wonderful!" Lady exclaimed. And all went back to their seats with the audience still cheering wanting more.

Coming off stage last, Lady stopped by each lady's table before they left to register for next Saturday's class. They had no idea that they helped her tremendously filling in for the lack of dancers for her show. But even more than that, Lady would now have a whole troupe that showed significant possibilities to go further than simply dancing in her restaurant. Her new troupe were diamonds in the rough, but not really rough at all. *I think that all four have a unique natural ability in belly dancing.* Lady thought about the order in which she could place them in a show. This was a little premature, but something about them all together just gave her renewed inspiration.

Thomas gave Seri a big twirling hug when she reached the table, sweeping her off her feet.

"Girl! You still got it! I'm so proud of you! Wait till your daughters see their mom drop it like it's supposed to be dropped! I taped you. Did you see me from up there?" he said, showing her the camera's playback of her performance.

"Did I do okay?" Seri asked, still slightly out of breath and a little flushed in the cheeks, hoping he wouldn't notice and that it would quickly pass. He noticed.

"Here, missy, drink some water to cool down a bit, and have a seat." He handed her a glass of water and made sure she drank at least half of it.

"Are you going to be all right? Let's just rest here for a few before we go." Some of the patrons of the restaurant stopped by their table to wish her well, and said that they hoped to see her soon again on stage in another show. Some said they couldn't believe that they just learned in that short of time to be so good. Seri and Tomas sat for a while longer enjoying the playback performance on his camera phone and decided to split a little fruit dessert cake.

Shylessa and Bird went right outside with the

other drummers. They were on break now and wanted to see the pictures and video Bird took of everything and themselves.

Funesta had the whole weekend off; that was a good move on her part. Now she was guessing what his next move would be after he gave her a flirtatious kiss on the hand when she returned from the stage and they sat side by side.

"You just wowed the audience and me too!" Afton said. "We have something in common." He took her hand again and kissed it softly. "We are both looking for that right person to share in our lives. I think I could be happy with what I have found tonight. I would like to get to know you, Funesta Flores, if you let me." He searched her eyes; then his gaze went to her lips. Her lips still had a gloss of color from her lipstick or her wine. Fixated with her lips he leaned over to taste them for himself.

Finally, Funesta thought as she closed her eyes to receive what she was waiting for all…night…a deep, deep kiss. She felt his mustache first on her top lip then on her bottom lip before he plunged in fully. Fun was not the type to kiss on the first date, but this time was not going to wait and get away from the electricity between them. She knew he felt it too.

Tesseanna was not as enthused with her date when she returned to her table. She could see that Rick was still messing with his phone. All of the red flags were there that she would normally break off a date swiftly, if not immediately, like checking his watch and cell phone on a date. She came to the conclusion that he was too much of a "fly guy" for her to deal with. So after a quick hug of congratulations on a good job from him, she finished most of her drink and listened to her inner self.

"I think we should call it a night," Tess said finally.

"What?" he snapped. A flash of anger was in his voice, but he quickly tried to cover it up and put the smoothness back in. Hoping she didn't notice he added, "I mean let's relax a little while longer so you can catch your breath. You were great up there; are you sure you're not a dancer? You remind me of a dancer at this strip club who gave me the idea of a belly dancer for my show in the first place." He saw the reaction on her face and realized that it was her. "It was you that night, wasn't it?! You're a stripper?"

"Yes, it was me, I work there as a waitress. They were short staffed that day. I just filled in to keep my job. I'm not a stripper!" she insisted, starting to get upset.

"No, you're not! You're my inspiration! Is this why you didn't tell me you worked there all this time? You thought I would prejudge you?" Rick said, knowing all along he wouldn't mind if she was a stripper. But he didn't tell her that.

"Yes, and now I know why you want me to 'dance' in your show." She made the little quote mark gesture in the air. "What you want is the name of a good stripper. I can help you with that." Tesseanna started to get up to leave.

"Wait! Tess, please." Rick stopped her by cupping her hand with his hands. "You didn't strip anyway. When I saw you dance, it was very classy and mysterious. The dance of the seven or more like twenty veils the way you did it. It was beautiful. You were pulling fabric out of midair like magic! Bottom line is that the hardcore audience loved it and you didn't even expose anything. I didn't even know it was you till just now. That crowd really liked it, as an artful not erotic expression of dancing. To me that says a lot!" He had her back seated in her seat.

"Well, I'd be lying if I said I wasn't shocked by the reaction I received that night. I thought for sure I would be booed for not taking it all off," Tess admitted and whispered, "I did have fun dancing."

"But now I know that you were the one danc-ing, I think that would be considered professional dancing and you would be disqualified from the show. So you are off the hook. But I hope we can still be good...friends." Knowing all the well he already had a girlfriend. Rick ordered another round of drinks for the two before leaving. Out in the parking lot, right before Rick opened the car door for Tess, he pulled her tight to him and kissed her, and she kissed him back. But not for long. Their kiss was interrupted by a nearby shout.

"Get your UGLY FACE OFF MY MAN!" It was Rick's girlfriend, Veronica, quickly walking toward the two.

"Veronica, what are you doing here? Are you following me?" A flare of anger in Rick's voice came up again.

"Hell yeah! Who's your new whore?" Veronica gave Tess the customary eye-rolling, disapprov-ing sneer of the mouth, hand on hip, head up and down, finger in the face look. She acted like she was going to do something until Tess stood up next to her, with at least a foot difference in Tess's favor. Veronica quickly turned her attention back to Rick before she got her weave snatched out.

Rick was busy keeping Tess away from Veronica. So he put Tess in his car, calming her down by telling her that it was a crazy ex-girlfriend, and they would leave right now. When he turned around after closing the door of the car, he was taken by surprise by a double slap across his face.

Veronica got him good, turned, and ran away crying and loudly cussing him out. Her ruckus was witnessed by patrons going to their cars. Shy, Bird, and the band members stopped looking at Bird's phone to eavesdrop on the commotion. Tess assumed she was through with him. She would be if she didn't need a ride back to her own car. Tess didn't believe that she was an ex-girlfriend but she thought he was truly officially single now. And no matter how fine he was, she was not going down that ugly path with him no matter what lies he came up with, trying to smooth over this first date's disastrous end. And it was coming to an end, as soon as she got back to her car, or an Uber was going to be called. When Rick got into the car he started the apologies just as she expected, but they fell on deaf ears. Only until he started to cry, not like a baby, just one tear and the wiggly voice. He must have seen this on TV thinking this might work on some girls, but not this girl. Tess held her thoughts to herself. Rick of course kept on trying to manipulate his way out.

Seconds passed by before the startling sound of screeching rubber tires and a revved-up engine pierced the silence. Headlights projected their glare across Tess and Rick's turning heads. Toward the back of the car, in the next instant, jarring metal on metal, twisting collision, screams and glass shattering sounds fills the air. In the opposing BMW, Veronica planned to ram the "cheating asshole's" car twice, but the airbag deployed, causing Veronica's foot to press harder on the gas pedal.

Seemingly in slow motion, but seconds, the patrons coming out of the Diamond Coins restaurant watched in horror as Veronica's car, sideswiping the whole length of his Audi, picked up speed, jumped the embankment of the parking lot, and rolled into the ravine, flipping upside down and coming to a stop. Screams from the crowd were punctuated by the police car sirens pulling up, thinking they only had a minor disturbance. The two police officers went immediately to the flipped car to check on the driver. One of the officers came up slowly shaking his head, calling for an ambulance and backup.

Seri and Thomas were still in the restaurant when they heard the sirens and screams coming from the front entrance, and decided it was time to get out of there. Seri stood up too fast, fainted from the rush of blood to her head. Thomas reached out as she was going down and got her chair under her just in time.

"Seri! Girl, don't start this shit again! BABY!"

Running out from the kitchen, Lady Amisi was on her way to see what in the world the sirens and yelling and screaming were that were going on in her establishment! Before she could make it to the front door she saw Seri, one of her new dancers, jump up and fall out of her seat; her husband caught her before she hit the floor, getting her back into her seated position. "What is going on, Seri, are you all right?!" Lady immediately darted over, heading for the couple.

"I'm okay." Seri batted her eyes. "I just stood up too fast. I'm good now." Thomas and Lady fanned Seri for a moment, watching her carefully.

"What is going on out front!" Lady asked, still hearing the sirens and crying. "You two rest here. I must see what is happening!"

Lady opened the door and a gasp escaped her! People and cops everywhere, car parts, a smashed car and... "Oh my God!" One car upside down and an ambulance pulling up.

The police cleared out all the witnesses and bystanders after questioning by the police and a look at the small cut on Tess's head by the paramedics that would no doubt leave a lump after her head hit the side passenger's window. They were free to leave. Not wanting to go to the hospital, Rick knew he would run into Veronica's grieving parents. He already knew that he lost his dream when they lost a daughter.

His car was okay to drive himself home, alone.

Shy and Bird drove Tess to her car. "Are you sure you're all right?" Shy offered to stay with her. Tess declined.

It was a quiet ride. When they got back to her car, she said good night and quickly got into her car and started it and pulled off for home. Blocking out everything else, all she could think of was that quick kiss as she went to sleep.

⤞❖⤝

The next morning, Bird, being the first name on the lease and the only twenty-one-year-old, received the approval notice for the apartment they applied for on her phone first. Bird had spent the night at Shylessa's house and woke her friend up with the news that they could move into the apartment in less than a week. Their happiness rang all through the whole house, which of course drew the attention of Shy's parents.

"You got WHAT!" Shy's mother and father said in perfect unison, and the shock on both faces matched with shock in finding out what all the ruckus was about. The information that their daughter had found an apartment and was moving out so suddenly was more than they could have guessed coming from their daughter's mouth. After the disbelief of what they heard, Mrs. Glasgow was the first to fire up.

"What about your education? And your piano students and their classes? And you have responsibilities to the praise dancers at church... that's too much. I think you need to cancel all of this nonsense right now! You're not ready for this kind of thing. And..." Before her mother could catch her breath for another round of let-downs, Shy stopped her in mid-sentence.

"NO! YOU'RE not ready! And we *are* moving on and out at the end of this week to a very nice two-bedroom apartment. Now you can help us, but do not hinder and that is that!"

Shylessa spoke with an undeniable, authoritative, takin' no bull, ain't havin' it voice to her mom and then turned her attention to her father. The look on her father's face was almost enough to make her burst out laughing. He had both hands covering up his eyes but was peeking out to see if the fireworks had started or not, peeking from mother to daughter.

Taking her father's hands down from his face and holding them, Shy calmed down and told him the news she knew he had been waiting for.

"The apartment is close to my choice of schools. I will be attending the U of M! I have finally decided," Shy said.

"I think that is a good choice," her father said, nodding to his wife, who was standing with her arms crossed in an unapproving stance.

"What about your piano classes and the praise dancers rehearsals?" he added, hoping she had thought of everything responsibly.

"I've been approved to teach piano at the church for a small monthly fee, and the praise dancers will rehearse in the basement there at the church from now on. That gives us more room anyway. But I will have to work it out with my class schedule to confirm any hours or dates," Shy said, looking at both of her parents now, poised for any more questions from either of them. Mrs. Glasgow couldn't decide whether to get mad or cry. She stood there for a moment looking at her daughter and husband, who was doing his best to edge her onto their side. She could see the determination in her daughter's face but she also could see something else.

A beautiful, intelligent, headstrong young woman, not the little girl needing protecting. This young woman and her best friend were just at the start of a new crossroad. She was not going to be left out of it.

"I can't stop you, so I will support you in your branching-out decision, any way I can," she said with tears welling up in her eyes.

"Yippee! Family hug!" Bird yelled out and brought all three together in a group hug. With that outburst tears and laughter filled the room.

After a few dance classes together as a new troupe, Diamond Coins began a close friendship together. Learning to put on a professional show as a troupe was a new challenge for all, and they each cheered each other on. They were more of a family than a troupe of dancers. Lady Amisi showed them the way to choreograph and sharpen their belly dancing skills at each class. And all of their classes had a warmup to start out with, then a brisk workout dance to burn calories, and then each had a special skill to work on followed by a cooldown and stretching out the muscles they didn't even know they had to end each session.

In a choreographed show there are distinctive stages of a belly dance show. There can be up to four and a finale. Lady liked to think of the stages like life. First, you're just starting out, dreamy, like the entrance. Second, you're coming out and starting to experience what life has to offer, setting the groundwork, just like unveiling and floor work. Third, you enjoy life and give it what you've got, just like the upbeat, feisty, and spirited dance with canes. Fourth, you have the experience and the power for the dynamic and much anticipated drum solo. With all of the stages together, you have fellowship with people who care about your journey through life like the combination of stages in the finale. Lady Amisi found it very easy to place each of her new dancers into the stage they belonged to. Shylessa would start off first with the entrance. Not only was she the youngest but she really knew how to show expression with the veil, and she could make the veil talk like it was truly an extension of her arm and herself.

Tesseanna's artistic unveiling put her second. A multitalented dancer able to master the double veil and floor work in a taxim's slower musical beat. She was mesmerizing to watch, a very polished dancer. But there was something going on in her life, and she was keeping it to herself. What, only time would tell. Funesta of course had that upbeat cane dance down pat now and was expanding to the use of the finger cymbals or zills as they are called. Not too different from snapping her fingers, dancing at all the parties she had attended. Full of energy and glowing in love, everyone could feel and see that from her dancing.

Seri was the serious drum soloist, showing off the unmatched power in her hips. Isolating energy in her hips seemed to come easily for her. Eating healthy and working out regularly had really worked for her and showed. She had lost more weight in the right areas and keeping the weight off lowered her blood pressure and gave her more energy.

As an extra bonus, Lady Bird, as a new drummer to the stage, added energy to the percussion section.

"Ladies, if I could have your attention please." Lady beckoned the practicing dancers in closer for a little talk. Once everyone was gathered around she began.

"I respectfully put in my bid to be the manager of the Diamond Coins Belly Dancing Troupe," Lady began and was immediately interrupted with whoops and yeehaahs! Going forward with approval, Lady would lead the new troupe.

"My direction for this troupe is clear to me. First we will rehearse for a play that I have in mind, and also for this spring, with more training we will enter the Golden Belly Awards as a troupe and bring home the trophy of Troupe of the Year!" Lady could almost feel the trophy in her hand.

❦

Losing was never easy for Swaysa. Her birth name was Virginia Sway; she never used that name anymore, but never had it officially changed. She came up with her new stage name by embellishing her last name after perfecting a swaying hip movement she liked.

Swaysa had always felt as though she danced in the shadows of Amisi, and this time she was not going to let her friend upstage her. Swaysa was going to be the star, this one moment in time.

Ever since they met in elementary school, Amisi Taylor stood out, always, like the teacher's pet type of girl. Amisi was always the one to be called on first in class. Swaysa wasn't sure if it was because Amisi was so trustworthy or she was so beautiful. Amisi had a beautiful golden-bronze skin tone; maybe she used too much lotion. Amisi also had huge doe-brown eyes and shiny jet-black hair; maybe she deep conditioned it too much. But there was no disputing the way Amisi's eyes smiled when she smiled, and even Swaysa found it hard to stay mad at Amisi. But it was still easy to be jealous of her. Swaysa and Amisi had become competitive "friends" over the years.

Swaysa and Amisi shared the passion for dance, all types of dance, starting with taking tap and jazz lessons together in elementary school. In middle school the only thing offered was ribbon and baton, if not in sports, so they were in that afterschool program together for a few years. In high school both made it into the cheerleading squad easily, together again.

Amisi was the first to find belly dancing classes within walking distance from where she lived, so she had a little more of a head start on the dance than Swaysa, by six months. But Amisi did invite her to join her. When Swaysa finally agreed to join her in a trial dance class, she loved it and never stopped. Swaysa mastered the dance and years later started her own belly dance company, the same year Amisi started her dance company.

Friends or not, a rivalry was always in play as far as Swaysa was concerned with Amisi. Competition, it was just that, who was the best.

Lady Amisi, her stage name, had a flair for the dramatic choreography with every prop, veil, zills, and of course the cane dance. Swaysa could excel on floor dance and her belly roll. She had command over every ab muscle she had and could move each separately to create quite the mesmerizing, dramatic effect. It was her attitude that she couldn't always control. Amisi was always there for her; even Swaysa would have to admit to that, if she had to.

The two dance companies along with other dance companies in the twin cities area held competitions or dance shows to raise money for the charity of their choice. The next competition was to be the title and golden trophy for The Golden Belly Awards coming up in the spring.

Swaysa had her troupe working on multiple numbers. But for once she, Swaysa, wanted to be the first. She wanted the title and the bragging rights to the golden trophy in her dance studio trophy case.

The past should stay in the past. That fall that broke Lady Amisi's hip and ankle when she was dancing all those years ago, still she was awarded and able to take home the elaborately adorned raks sharqui dress that was the prize for that year's competition. How did she fall? What caused her to fall? Water under the bridge now. They gave Amisi the dress anyway, and it hung in her restaurant entrance for all to enjoy.

Swaysa had just finished her dance that night right before Lady Amisi took the stage, and there might have been a couple of beads from her homemade hip scarf left on the stage after Swaysa finished, maybe, or it could have just been glitter that she saw sparkling on the stage when she took her bow.

"Glitter, yeah, that's it," Swaysa conveniently concluded. Swaysa and the Swaying Gems—the winners! That was what Swaysa wanted more than anything.

Lady Amisi just might just step back onto the stage once again. Spring was always a new beginning.

Not the end, just the beginning.

Afterword

At the begininning of the day, in their cars, at a four way intersection, four women wait for each to take their turn. Each at a different crossroad in their lives. Missing something, just living day to day.

That is what each one has in common with one another. Dance has a nice way of bringing total strangers together for the benefit of all involved. Life as a bellydance. Either fighting the fight with weight loss or achieving fitness goals for medical reasons like blood pressure or heart health. Low impact stress reliever, or just the basic feelings of just wanting to feel good about themselves and more energy. Dance. Namaste from one soul to another.

CPSIA information can be obtained
at www.ICGtesting.com
Printed in the USA
BVHW041642150421
605035BV00008B/560

9 781977 234230